GOL[E]

JO[

The Murail siblings are all hugely successful authors in their own right – Marie-Aude has sold over two million books worldwide, Elvire's very first novel was turned into a film and Lorris is well known for writing about his two passions: good food and science fiction. Together they make a truly formidable literary trio. When writing the Golem series, the siblings wanted not only to recapture the intensity and creativity of playing together as children, but also to write the kinds of books they would have liked when they were young. "It was like a game," says Elvire, the youngest. "It was a huge challenge, but we wanted to lose our individual voices and morph into a new, even better one. It worked so well that sometimes we had trouble remembering who had written what!" Her sister Marie-Aude adds, "It's so important to remember what you were like when you were young. It gets more difficult as you get older – you have to have your own children to get it back again!" It took two years to complete all five Golem books.

Now it is your turn to play…

GOLEM

This book is supported by the French Ministry for Foreign Affairs, as part of the Burgess programme headed for the French Embassy in London by the Institut Français du Royaume-Uni.

Liberté • Égalité • Fraternité
RÉPUBLIQUE FRANÇAISE

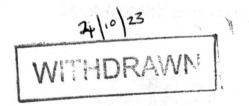

Golem

2: Joke

Elvire, Lorris and Marie-Aude Murail
translated by Sarah Adams

WALKER BOOKS
AND SUBSIDIARIES
LONDON · BOSTON · SYDNEY · AUCKLAND

First published 2005 by Walker Books Ltd
87 Vauxhall Walk, London SE11 5HJ

2 4 6 8 10 9 7 5 3 1

Original Edition: *Golem 2 – Joke*
© 2002 Éditions Pocket Jeunesse,
division of Univers Poche, Paris – France
English translation © 2005 Sarah Adams
Cover image © 2005 Guy McKinley

This book has been typeset in DeadHistory and M Joanna

Printed and bound in Great Britain
by Bookmarque Ltd, Croydon, Surrey

British Library Cataloguing in Publication Data:
a catalogue record for this book
is available from the British Library

ISBN 1-84428-615-0

www.walkerbooks.co.uk

Contents

In Golem: LEVEL 1:

0%

10%

20%

30%

40%

50%

60%

70%

80%

90%

Majid Badach has just won a state-of-the-art computer and he and his teacher, Hugh, are obsessed with a pirate game that keeps hijacking their screens. Using their gamer names of Magic Berber and Calimero, they get to explore amazing graphics and design the creature of their dreams.

But strange things are happening on Majid's estate. The electricity keeps failing, Aisha witnesses smoke on the landing, and little Lulu suddenly gets up out of her sickbed. Samir and Sebastian have a narrow escape from a thing in the basements, but the delivery man from Price Shrinkers isn't so lucky — he's found dead down there, covered in burn marks.

And now Golem seems to have taken on a life of its own: Majid's printer has just turned itself on and spewed out a sheet, reading:

Play, Magic Berber, play.
I'm Waiting for you.

... 100%

››Transfer complete

—

START PLAY ››

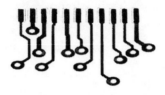

Where's Chechnya?

The small van was hurtling towards the Moreland Estate. Inside it were a journalist and her cameraman. There was no time to waste. They had to file the report by 8 p.m.

"Aren't people fed up with stories about mashed-up estates?" asked Momo the cameraman. "There was one last week about joyriders in Rokaz. And yesterday it was kids staging a hold-up in a grocery store in Fester—"

Emily Barter cut him short. "Compared with Chechnya, this is a holiday."

"Yeah, well, when you look at it that way," he said grudgingly. "So, what's the story?"

"The police received an anonymous phone call about a body in the basements of Hummingbird Tower on the Moreland Estate. They followed up the lead, and that's exactly what they found. But there was no ID."

"Usual story," said Momo, who'd seen everything after twenty years of filming news reports.

"But it hots up because the guy had burn marks all over his body."

Momo smacked his lips. "Now *that's* more like it. Are we talking torture in the basements? Kids killing time? We'll have to find out if the residents heard any cries for help." He was hungry for a scoop. They'd grill the losers in this dump and land themselves an exclusive. *They heard him screaming in the night. Now they're afraid to leave their homes. Who will be next?*

He started whistling. They might even get the headline slot. The newsreader would look directly into the camera and say darkly: "Spring's in the air, but there's panic on the streets."

When he saw the grey concrete towers of the Moreland Estate sticking up against the sky, Momo scowled. Not very photogenic. He slowed down level with two boys playing football. "Hey, guys! Which is Hummingbird Tower?"

The older boy came over to the van. "It's the TV!" he shouted to his younger brother. "Have you come about the murder?"

"Got it in one," said Momo. "So where's this Hummingbird Tower?"

"Can we have your autograph?" asked the older brother.

"He's not famous," scoffed the younger one. "You ever seen him on TV?"

The cameraman tapped the steering wheel. Some people around here needed a kick up the backside. "Are you going to tell me or not?"

The older brother explained at great length. "On the right, see the second building over there? Well, it's not that one. You take a left."

Momo frowned as he repeated the instructions, then set off without bothering to thank them. The kids waited for the van to disappear before knocking their fists together. "Touch, blud!"

They'd sent Momo in the wrong direction.

Fifteen minutes later, the van was back.

"This place is starting to get on my nerves," Momo complained. "If I land on those kids again…"

"They didn't just lose us in Chechnya," Emily reminded him, "they kidnapped us into the bargain."

"Yeah, well, when you look at it that way," he grunted. "Hold on a minute, let's ask Grandad over there… 'Scuse me!"

Grandad dragged his wolfhound over to the van. He was suspicious at first but soon broke into a broad smile. The TV!

"We're looking for Hummingbird Tower."

"Well, you've come to the right person," said Grandad. "I'm the caretaker."

Emily and Momo glanced at each other. They wanted Grandad on camera.

"Would you mind if we asked you a few questions?" said the journalist.

"Don't I have to be made up for the TV?"

Emily nearly laughed in the old man's face. "No, we don't bother for the news."

They decided to set up in front of Hummingbird Tower. Momo lifted the camera onto his shoulder while Emily started the interview.

"You're the caretaker of Hummingbird Tower. Did you ever think a murder would happen here?"

"To be honest with you," the caretaker replied, "anything could happen round here. Just take Brutus."

"Who?"

"My dog."

Momo re-angled the camera to film the wolfhound.

"He had a funny turn on the night of the murder," said Grandad. "He always pees just here on this bollard, opposite the main entrance" – we're going to have to edit that bit out, thought Emily – "but he was edgy that evening. Growling, his eyes rolling… Strange that, because he's regular as clockwork is our Brutus. Always pees bang on time, on the bollard—"

"Fine," Emily interrupted. "But what about you? Did you notice anything suspicious that night?"

"To be honest with you, there's been all these power cuts. The lift keeps breaking down, the bulbs keep going. Twenty years I've been caretaker here. Never seen anything like it. You put in a brand-new bulb and *pop*, it goes just like that!"

Momo sighed and lowered the camera. Grandad was a basket case. Ask him about a murder and he started talking about the national grid.

Just then a pretty West African girl walked out of Hummingbird Tower.

"Hey!" Momo called out.

Aisha went up to them shyly.

"D'you live in this building?" asked Emily. "Would you mind answering a few questions?"

"It's for the TV," Momo added, as if he was trying to bribe a toddler with a bag of sweets.

"I don't know if I'm allowed to," Aisha stammered. She'd been brought up strictly and her dad might blast her for talking to a stranger. Then again, it was for TV...

Emily started the interview regardless. Momo resumed filming.

"So you live in Hummingbird Tower. Did you know a dead body's been found in the basements? Have you noticed anything suspicious lately?"

"Yes," answered Aisha, looking away. "There's smoke floating around on my landing. And it sends out sparks."

Momo groaned and put the camera down again.

"Wait, we might be on to something," said Emily. "Where do you think this smoke is coming from? Are there kids messing about with fire?"

"No!" Aisha panicked. "No way! It's smoke without fire. It's the spirits of dead people coming back to visit us."

"They're all basket cases here!" declared Momo, switching off his camera.

"Let's try one more," sighed Emily.

The journalist and her cameraman loitered around until they noticed a boy trying to see how far he could spit. He was of North African origin and looked about ten years old. As soon as Momo started filming, the boy posed self-consciously with his baseball cap on back to front.

"Ra-aa-ah!" he said when asked about the dead body. Then he broke into Moreland Estate back-slang. "There's nuff scary stuff going down ing-Humm-turd wer-To."

We'll have to use subtitles, thought Emily.

"What kind of stuff?" she asked.

"Me bro's bluds hang with the 8D crew, innit. An' dey is biggin' it up, like, 'bout a ghost in ing-Humm-turd ment-bases."

"Basket cases, the lot of them." Momo shook his head.

Emily signalled to him to be quiet. "What exactly do you mean by *ghost*?"

"Well, like a ghost, you get me?" answered the boy, looking at Emily as if she was a moron from Year 4. "Like a white thing with sheets. But the land-More ghost is dern-mo coz it makes electricity. It's like an tric-elec ghost, you get me?"

Emily finally lost heart. "Let's drop it," she said to Momo.

They walked away from Hummingbird Tower. Before climbing back into the van the cameraman trod in a big mound of dog poo. He scraped his shoe against Brutus's favourite bollard. "What a dump," he muttered under his breath. "Are we out of here?"

But Emily didn't give up on assignments so easily. She decided to drop by the police station. It turned out to be a glorified hut hidden at the end of an overgrown garden. The journalist found a young officer wearing trainers, who seemed to have escaped the madness of the Moreland Estate.

"The corpse?" he repeated. "We don't know who he is. He didn't have any papers on him."

"Nothing that might help identify him?" Emily asked while Momo filmed.

"We've made some progress with the investigation, since the tub of farting goo."

Emily thought she must have misheard. "The tub of...?"

"Farting goo." The young officer giggled. "You know, you press it and it makes ... noises ... sound effects. The dead man had a tub of it in his left pocket."

Emily was worried now. Farting goo was a no-go area for TV news.

"They're saying it's a special kind," the officer added in a "between you and me" sort of voice. "Not available in the shops yet. A prototype."

Emily's laugh was faintly hysterical. Prototype farting goo. This was getting insane.

Back in the van, Momo had a confession to make. "You know what? I preferred Chechnya."

Now That's What
I Call Manners

The caretaker of Hummingbird Tower couldn't take much more. Dead bodies, TV crews, kids breaking the lifts – who else could it be? And as if that wasn't enough, a huge green rubbish skip had been parked right opposite the main entrance for the last month. Everybody used it to dump their broken fridges and cookers, not to mention their sagging old mattresses with the springs poking out. Which in turn attracted homeless types. Some guy had set up camp there yesterday evening.

"What's going on now?" the caretaker grumbled, seeing two men emerging from the basements. "The police again?"

He didn't go over. He'd had enough of being interrogated, thank you. So he just watched them talking and looking worried. One was tall and skinny. The other was younger with totally white hair and an albino's complexion. If they'd turned up to a casting for the baddies in the next *Lethal Weapon*, they'd have been hired on the spot. And if Majid had been there, he'd have recognized the delivery men from Price Shrinkers who'd tried to get his computer back off him.

The two men headed over.

"Hello," said Chalk Face. "Are you the caretaker?"

"We're looking for something. It's to do with the murder," Skinny Bloke added.

"I've already been questioned," objected the caretaker. "I've said everything I've got to say. Well, actually I didn't say anything because I've nothing to say. Didn't see anything, didn't hear anything. Are you from the police?"

"Not … exactly," said Chalk Face.

"Private detectives?" asked the caretaker, who'd read a few detective stories in his youth.

"Yeah, that's right, private detectives," Skinny

Bloke agreed. "We've been hired by a woman looking for her husband. He walked off with the cheque book, get it?"

The caretaker didn't get it at all, but he pretended he'd followed every word.

"We're wondering if the body in the basements might be the husband," said Chalk Face. "What did he look like?"

The caretaker shuddered. The police had made him go and see the corpse in the morgue, for identification purposes. "It's hard to say," he mumbled. "He was tall. Burn marks all over. Even on his face."

The two men gave each other a tense look.

"Clothes?"

"They were burnt too."

"Nothing in the pockets?"

"No. Oh, yes! A tub of farting goo. A special one, or that's what I was told."

The two men winced. It was Sven all right.

"Nothing else?" said Chalk Face. "No mobile?"

The caretaker shook his head. No mobile.

The news seemed to be a blow.

"Does the mobile matter?"

Chalk Face tried to brush it off. "No, it was a contract phone, that's all. Just making sure nobody else uses it…"

They thanked the caretaker, slipped him some cash and drove off in their khaki jeep.

Now that's what I call manners, thought the caretaker, not realizing he'd just met a pair of hired killers.

The homeless man in the rubbish skip had watched the scene with interest. "We meet again," he said under his breath when he spotted Chalk Face.

He was an unusual-looking tramp, tall, badly shaven, with dark shadows under his eyes. His jacket was stained and creased, and he wasn't wearing a tie. He looked like a senior executive who'd recently been sacked and had run to seed. But a feverish glow in his eyes hinted otherwise. This man was a survivor.

"We meet again," he repeated as he spied on the fake delivery men.

They weren't here by coincidence. He wasn't the only one on the computer's trail. From his pocket, the strange tramp took a piece of paper ripped out of a mail-order catalogue. There was the photo of Majid and his mum in front of their handsome New Generation BIT computer. *Mrs Badach and her son Majid (Moreland Estate), happy winners of our Price Shrinkers competition.*

"Happy winners!" The man smirked. "They certainly hit the jackpot." He screwed up his eyes to get a closer look at the photo that had put him back on the trail. He didn't need a magnifying glass to recognize his computer with its electric blue shell, the only New Generation BIT machine that colour, but what he was trying to glimpse was what was on the computer's screen.

"Golem," he whispered.

Five black letters could be made out against a red background: **Golem**. A brilliant computer game and a nasty piece of work. There. He'd said it. A nasty piece of work. But how had that kid Majid managed to tap into Golem when there were codes protecting it? He must be some kind of computer wizard.

Up at the Badachs', Majid had no idea somebody in the rubbish skip twelve floors down had such a high opinion of him. He'd just placed a present in front of his mum.

"Happy birthday, Emmay!"

Emmay pretended to be surprised, as she did every year. "Iz for me?"

"Go on, open it," her husband encouraged her.

Emmay looked from husband to youngest son. For a moment, she nearly burst into tears. She'd had seven sons, and all seven were handsome, healthy young men. But where were the other six this evening?

"Oh, iz very nice idea!" she gushed when she opened it.

"It was my idea," said Majid.

Emmay gave her son and her husband a kiss. What she really wanted for her birthday were her seven sons. What she'd got was another electric kettle.

"And now for the *real* surprise," said Majid. He and his dad had been keeping it a secret for the last three days.

"You and I are going out to dinner at a restaurant," announced Mr Badach.

Emmay thought he was joking.

"You only get one birthday a year," her husband insisted. "You don't want to miss out." Mr Badach didn't say so, but he knew that working like he had to raise seven sons, he'd missed out on their first steps seven times, their first words seven times too. And he didn't like to count how many birthdays he'd missed. So, for once, Mr and Mrs Badach were going to celebrate in style.

"Just the two of you, how romantic!" teased Majid.

"Why don't you wear your favourite dress?" Mr Badach added.

Emmay only wore her favourite dress on special occasions. And the restaurant counted as one. She was also going to wear the gold necklace she'd kept hidden inside a saucepan ever since she'd received it as a wedding gift. As well as the earrings she liked to stuff in her socks: a present from her mother-in-law.

"You're more beautiful than a princess!" Mr Badach declared when he saw Mrs Badach in her dress with garish red poppies splashed all over it. She looked curvy and golden and she was jangling with jewellery.

Mr Badach was right. But Majid was getting

impatient. He wanted his parents off his case. Golem was waiting.

"You iz sensible, Majid?"

"Yeah, yeah."

As soon as the door closed behind them, he went over to his computer.

Majid, aka Magic Berber, had been a bit scared of his machine ever since the printer had started working by itself. But at the same time, he was desperate to create his own golem.

Mr Badach came back in. He'd forgotten the car keys. It was Emmay's turn next. She wanted to change handbags. Then she had to change her shoes, to match her bag. Majid decided to wait a while before switching on the computer. When the doorbell rang, he congratulated himself. It was probably Emmay wanting to wear her shawl instead of her jacket.

"What's it this tim—"

He didn't get a chance to finish. Chalk Face grabbed him by the throat and forced him backwards. Skinny Bloke kicked the door shut. Majid tried struggling but that hand was choking him.

"Nice of your parents to make this easy for us!" Chalk Face laughed. "The computer, George. Get a move on."

George rushed at the equipment, ripping out the plugs in his haste. Majid was still trying to get out of Chalk Face's stranglehold, but the man had a firm grip and seemed to be amused by Majid's attempts to break free.

"What are we going to do with him?" asked George.

Chalk Face stuck his face in Majid's and puffed his bad breath right at him. "Nothing," he said. "Because the kid knows when to shut it, right?"

A strangled yes came from Majid's lips.

"Keep your mouth shut and we won't be back. Or we could just cut your tongue out here and now."

George chuckled and picked up the computer. Blimey! Not as light as it looked, this machine.

The front door hadn't been shut properly. It looked to Majid as if it was opening again. He saw a hand stealing through the gap. A hand holding a gun. He thought it was the third Shrinker coming to finish him off. George's feet had got tangled in the wires and he didn't notice the intrusion. Chalk Face had his back to the door.

Majid watched the man enter like a movie character in slow motion. The intruder raised his arm slowly and brought it down like lightning. *Whack* went the barrel of the gun as it cracked against Chalk Face's skull. Majid fell to the ground with him but managed to free himself from Chalk Face's grip. He was choking and terror-stricken. George couldn't move because he was still lumbered with the computer. The man was pointing the gun at him.

"Put the computer down!" he ordered.

George hesitated.

"Put it down."

George did as he was told.

"Turn round."

George hesitated again, guessing what was about to happen.

"Make it snappy!"

The man wasn't joking. George did as he was told. Only to be knocked senseless like his colleague. His assailant put his gun in his pocket before looking at Majid for the first time. "You OK?"

Majid had taken refuge in the corner, his back against the Babar wallpaper. He was scared stiff.

"D'you have any string?" the man asked. "I've got to tie them up so I can get rid of them for you."

Majid peeled himself away from the wall. Get rid of them? And what about him? What was the man going to do with him? "There's some in the kitchen," he whispered.

"Fetch!" said the man, as if he was talking to his dog.

No point arguing with somebody who'd got a gun in his pocket. Majid went into the kitchen and came back with a ball of string.

The intruder pulled a face. "That stuff's for tying up the Sunday roast… Well, I guess I'm just going to have to truss them up."

For a moment, Majid thought about running away while the man was busy. Could he make it to Aisha's flat opposite?

"I'm not going to hurt you," said the man, second-guessing him. "I'm … I'm Albert." He introduced himself as if he'd just decided something. Chances were it wasn't his real name.

"Listen, Majid. That's your name, isn't it? Good. Now, you've got yourself mixed up in some funny business. You have to do exactly what I tell you. The computer can't stay here. They'll be back. These guys, or more like them."

"From Price Shrinkers?"

"From where? Oh no! They're not from Price Shrinkers." Albert started laughing while he was trussing up Chalk Face like a joint of roast beef. Then he looked up and his feverish eyes stared into Majid's. "Now, listen carefully. You've got to move the computer to a safe place. A hideout. I can't look after it. I've got to find somewhere to hide myself."

"But what if they come back and interrogate me?" Majid panicked.

"Tell them I took it with me. Tell them I stole it. D'you understand, Majid? They mustn't get their hands on this machine *at any price*. There's something inside it. It's not an ordinary computer."

"Yeah, I noticed that."

Albert interrupted his trussing operation to look curiously at Majid. He'd forgotten he was dealing with a computer wizard. "So how'd you get into Golem?" he asked.

"I didn't do anything!" Majid protested. "It came to me. Even the printer started working by itself. It wants me to play."

"Don't play any more!" roared Albert. He didn't know how the game had got so out of hand. There was something wrong. He asked for a roll of tape and gagged the two men. George was starting to loosen the string.

"Call up the lift," Albert barked.

Majid did as he was told. That man knew how to give orders. If he'd said "jump out of the window", Majid wouldn't have hesitated. The lift was having one of its good days, and it made it all the way up to the twelfth floor. Albert dragged the two men inside. Then he gave Majid a long hard stare. Was it too much of a risk leaving him like this?

"Don't tell anybody," he said. "Not a word to the police or your parents. Your life depends on it. I'll get in touch as soon as I can." He pressed the button for the ground floor, and a flicker of a smile appeared on his tired face. "Golem's some game, hey?"

The door closed. Majid wasn't sure, but he thought Albert might have added, "I invented it."

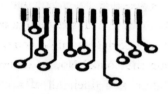

Golem in the Library

Majid hid in his wardrobe, waiting for his parents to get back. When he heard the front door bang, followed by the sound of Emmay's voice, he slipped into bed. He knew his mum would come in to check on him, so he pretended to be asleep. But he didn't drop off until the small hours.

He had a few things on his mind. One, he'd nearly been killed by a pair of delivery men who, it turned out, weren't delivery men at all. Two, the man who'd rescued him, Albert, was as terrifying as the men who'd attacked him. Three, there was something inside his computer. Something highly dangerous and sought after. Something. But what? A bomb? A microfilm? Or else… The electric smoke that Aisha had seen. The horrible white thing in the basements. What if it was that? Well, if it was, then it wasn't inside the computer any more. It was on the loose.

Majid wondered if he should tell his parents, even though Albert had specifically ordered him not to. The fake Shrinkers might come back. What about alerting the police? No, no chance now he'd got a reputation as a thief. All of a sudden Majid thought of Sebastian. Aisha had told him Sebastian was an expert on ghosts and the living dead. Maybe a kid who was top of his class would know how to deactivate a bomb as well.

With all these worries and questions going round in his head, Majid didn't hear his alarm when it went off at seven o'clock the next morning.

The library – which had been expanded to include a multimedia lab and was now officially known as the integrated resources centre – was buzzing as usual during the lunch hour at Moreland School. Miss Minx, the school librarian, was tidying magazines and journals away into filing cabinets. In her mid-thirties, she still dressed like a teenager, wearing her hair in a plait that reached below her waist, and skirts that were too short for her but a hit with 10C.

"Quiet please!" she shouted automatically. "We're here to work!" Miss Minx knew that two thirds of the students were there to play on the computers. But she still hoped the remaining third were researching homework assignments. Actually, they just liked short skirts. "If you need to talk, please do so without shouting!" she shouted.

There were a lot of 8Ds in today, and they certainly weren't big readers. She tried to appear strict as she glanced around. Seeing Samir with his nose in a book, she smiled in surprise. Miss Minx was always telling her students how one day *each and every one of them* would find a book they liked. Samir must have found his. Out of curiosity, she peered over his shoulder. *The Canterville Ghost*. An excellent short novel.

"Are you enjoying it?"

Samir slammed the book shut. "Boring! It doesn't even teach you about ghosts. And there's no holy water."

Miss Minx was about to defend Oscar Wilde, when she heard a lot of noise coming from the computer area.

"Ra-aa-ah!" bellowed Mamadou.

"Shut it, fool," warned Zeinul.

Too late. Miss Minx was heading their way, followed by Samir. When she saw a little man in a helmet using a flame-thrower against a dragon, she knew that what was on the screen wasn't an educational program.

"What are you doing?"

"Nothing, miss!" said Mamadou. "It just appeared by itself."

"Of course it did," agreed the librarian. "And I'm the pope."

"You're prettier, miss," Mamadou reassured her.

Miss Minx pressed DEL in exasperation. The dragon reduced the warrior to ashes. **Burnt!** flashed up on the screen.

"Aargh, man!" fumed Mamadou. "You made me lose."

But the game was still there, and it was suggesting:

➤ start play
➤ end play

Miss Minx chose the second option. The game disappeared, but the blob-shaped white golem that Hugh called Joke installed itself in the middle of the screen, like a demonstrator blocking traffic. The librarian got increasingly annoyed as she tried pressing half the keys without any success.

"You're not meant to do that, miss!" Zeinul warned her.

Fatal error flashed up.

"See, now you've gone and crashed it," said Mamadou, feeling smug. "You'll have to switch it off and reboot it, miss."

Which was what Miss Minx did. But Fatal error flashed up once more.

"Like totally crashed it," muttered Mamadou, who wasn't feeling so smug after all.

Miss Minx had a very short fuse when it came to computers. "Right, 8D, find yourselves a book and keep quiet! I want to see everybody reading. Samir, get another book and sit down."

Samir was still staring at the screen, terrified.

He'd just seen the flabby blob Majid called a golem.

The librarian shook him by the shoulders. "Are you listening to me?"

Samir shrugged her off violently. "Lemme go! Geddoff!"

Miss Minx gave him an exasperated look but backed down. He had a real attitude problem, that one.

Just before afternoon lessons, Samir went looking for Sebastian and spotted him coming out of the toilets. He pushed him back inside roughly.

"Hey," Sebastian complained. "I don't need to go back in – I've just come out!"

"Shut it. I've got something to tell you."

Gangster style, Samir checked the joint was deserted by kicking all the cubicle doors open. Then he turned back to Sebastian. "You're not going to believe me," he whispered, "but remember that thing we saw in the basements? Well, it's the thing I saw on Majid's computer. And I've just seen it again in the library."

"In the library?"

"Scaled down, on the computer. A white blob

that just pops up on the screen. It's the same shape as the thing in the basements." Or the same lack of shape. Samir sketched a big lump in the air that flared out towards the bottom.

Sebastian frowned, as if he was checking the files in his head. "It turns up spontaneously on screens? I've read about that somewhere…"

While Samir waited patiently for the expert's verdict, he turned away two Year 7s. "Go play some place else," he told them in a tone of voice you don't argue with.

Sebastian's face lit up at last. "OK, I've got it. It's called transcommunication."

"Never heard of it," said Samir unenthusiastically. "So wassit mean, this trans-doodah business?"

"It's a method adopted by dead people to talk to the living. They use video players, phones and TVs to send their messages. I've got a book about it with lots of photos. You can see dead people's faces on a TV screen. It's been proved."

"I'm not getting the link."

Sebastian tried concentrating hard again. He was going to have to find a link just to shut Samir up. "The monster in the basements is a soul in pain.

It's trying to communicate with us. It wants us to help it."

"To do what?"

"To escape the middle level and rejoin the higher plane." Sebastian was more confident now. He'd read about it loads of times. It hadn't just been proved, it was actually rather straightforward as paranormal stuff went. "Look, it's stuck here. It's got to pay for a crime. It's like a punishment. Which explains why the holy water we threw at it had that effect."

"It does?"

Miss Minx would have been happy to take advantage of Sebastian's expertise. But she had to make do with the school caretaker, who happened to be into IT and had come to mend her computer. Unfortunately there was nothing he could do to get rid of Golem.

"You must have opened an email," he told her. "And this game was in it. It's like a virus."

Which explained why Golem had already infected three other computers in the integrated resources centre. It wasn't always on the screen, but it popped up several times a day. The students had quickly spotted it, of course, and in no time they were trying to outsmart the traps of Golemia, Golem City and Golem-Okh. The more they played, the more the game seemed to take root. After the caretaker had declared it to be a virus, Miss Minx banned it, threatened punishments, explained her reasons, argued, negotiated, and finally gave in. She was fed up. She had to turn crowds of students away every lunch hour and listen to cheers of "Go for it!" followed by indignant choruses of "What now?" And it looked like she was going to have to get used to it.

Luckily, there was a bug in Golem, which meant that even the hard-core tech-heads from 10C got stuck in a hotel room or a prison, and didn't know how to get out.

On Friday afternoon, the students of 7B were choosing their book of the month in the library.

"Give it back!"

Miss Minx looked round to see where the shouting had come from.

"I told you, I don't want to swap it!" whined

a waif-like girl, on the verge of tears.

The librarian immediately leapt to the girl's defence. A clear case of a small kid being picked on by a bigger one. "Give the book back at once, Kevin!"

Kevin and Naima looked at Miss Minx in confusion.

"What book?" asked Kevin.

"The one she doesn't want to swap."

The 7Bs who were near by started giggling.

"It isn't a book, miss," one of them said. "It's FG."

"It's mine," Naima snivelled.

Kevin sighed and took a tub of farting goo out of his pocket.

"I've FOR-BID-DEN students to swap that ... um ... er ... goo in my library," shouted Miss Minx in her strictest voice. "Hand it over, Kevin."

Naima burst into tears.

Miss Minx waited ten minutes after the bell had rung for the end of school, until there wasn't a sound in the corridors. Then she went over to her desk and opened a deep drawer. Inside were twenty tubs of farting goo with different-coloured lids. It was weird, and she'd never have owned up to the fact, but Miss Minx was crazy about farting goo. She'd got regular FG, fluorescent FG and scented FG.

"Banana ... banana..." whispered the librarian as she examined all the labels.

No, she hadn't confiscated that kind before. It must be a rare one. She put it with the other scented tubs: vanilla and lily of the valley. Then she locked her drawer again.

Life Isn't Always a Bunch of Roses

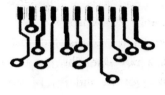

Hugh Mullins was enjoying a free Friday afternoon at home. No marking. Even better, no Samir or Mamadou. Hugh could give Golem his undivided attention. He'd never come across a game like it. He'd managed to outsmart the bug in the hotel room that was currently baffling the 10C tech-heads. Not that he knew what was going on in the integrated resources centre. He was more interested in the fact he'd managed to transform a pile of flashing pixels into a golem. A girl-golem.

"Well, *hello* there!"

Natasha had just popped up on his screen. Her curvaceous figure appeared several times a day (and night). All you had to do was click on her, and she pouted seductively and offered a sexy "Well, *hello* there!" The first time it had taken Hugh by surprise. Now it made him laugh.

"Hi," he answered.

Natasha waved at him before putting her hand back on her hip. She looked very fetching in her tiny shorts and figure-hugging strappy top which emphasized her disproportionately large chest. There were just two drawbacks. One, she had a weapon which Hugh called her eraser-laser slung across her shoulder. Two, she was virtual.

Hugh had worked out that he could launch the game by double-clicking on Natasha. The girl-golem now had a variety of different special powers. She had a sixth sense to detect enemy presence, invincible armour (to be used three times for up to twenty seconds) and a first-aid kit. She could see in the dark and walk through walls. He had also wanted to choose *ability to breathe underwater* and *good cook*, but those options didn't exist. Then again, Natasha had become a black belt in karate. And she had an *aggressive* personality. Hugh had done everything he could to select *obedient*, which seemed a good idea if not for a woman then at least for a golem. But, curiously, his commands had been blocked after *aggressive*. So Hugh found himself dealing with a warmongering girl-golem who made enthusiastic use of her eraser-laser.

The gamer was represented by the small helmeted warrior. To start with, Hugh had identified with the warrior. But now it annoyed him as much as if it was a rival.

"Well, *hello* there!"

Sometimes Natasha annoyed him too. When she seemed like just another girl making fun of him. Not only that, but the game itself made Hugh very tense. He hadn't worked out how to get beyond the closed room. And hordes of monsters were still waiting to ambush Natasha behind the door. The only time Hugh had clicked on the door, Natasha had died such a gruesome death he broke into a cold sweat just thinking about it.

Mrs Mullins knocked on another closed door. Her son's. "Don't you ever hear the phone, Hugh?"

He tore himself reluctantly away from the screen.

"That game has a hypnotic effect on you," his mother remarked.

Hugh mumbled something along the lines of "It's not the game that's the problem" and slouched into the sitting room.

"Hello, Thugh," said an attractive voice on the other end.

"Hi, Thad— Nadia." Without meaning to, Hugh had started copying the science teacher's lisp.

"You haven't forgotten about my little celebwation?" she said.

"Of course ... *not!*"

Nadia was having a party at four o'clock in the staffroom to celebrate her promotion from newly qualified teacher to permanent member of staff. She'd made some sangria because she'd noticed Hugh couldn't cope with alcohol. When he had a glass of wine, he started making risqué jokes. By the second glass he was chatting people up. And that was exactly what Nadia was waiting for. For Hugh to chat her up.

"A glass of sangwia?" she offered as soon as Hugh set foot inside the staffroom.

He shook his head. He'd got a headache from staring at Natasha on his screen.

"It's hardly got any alcohol in it," Nadia lied, thrusting a plastic cup into his hand.

The conversation was hotting up among the teachers. Miss Minx was talking about her computer problems in the library. "It's a virus, apparently," she explained to Mrs Cure, the tiny maths teacher. "It's a game you get sent by email, and then you can't get rid of it."

"Oh yes, I think I read something about it in a newspaper somewhere," said Mrs Cure. "What's the game called?"

"Golem."

Hugh's sangria nearly went down the wrong way. Having been unable to find Golem for sale anywhere, he'd got used to the idea that it only existed on his and Majid's screens. But now here it was popping up in the library and the national press.

"A little top-up?" Nadia suggested, filling his glass to the brim.

"Thanks. Not too much! Not too much! Um … you're looking very attractive today, Nadia." Hugh blushed deeply. He wasn't used to paying compliments.

"Just today?" she said, tilting her head coyly.

Hugh's eyes bulged. Nadia–Natasha. He'd just made the connection. Of course! They looked alike. Blonde, green eyes, a slightly provocative expression. One had inspired the other. He downed his second glass. He needed some Dutch courage. But by the time he'd psyched himself up, his place had already been taken. The PE teacher, who didn't need to be tipsy before he started chatting up the opposite sex, was trying his luck with Nadia. Hugh scowled and emptied two more glasses before noticing that the carpet was changing shape. Since nobody else seemed too concerned about it, he concluded logically enough that he was drunk and headed home unsteadily.

Back in his study, he clicked on Natasha.

"Well, hello there!"

Calimero stared at what he'd created until his eyes filled with tears. Why couldn't life be virtual? Then you could lasso dragons and blow-up PE teachers with your eraser-laser. It'd be so much less stressful than real life.

Albert might well have agreed with Hugh. He was sitting in front of a plate of sausages and chips, contemplating the fact that he'd had about as much as he could take of real life this past week. The two fake delivery men from Price Shrinkers had weighed a ton. Fortunately all the residents of Hummingbird Tower had been glued to their TV screens. Albert had managed to lug Chalk Face and Skinny Bloke to their khaki jeep without anybody noticing.

He'd thrown the most dangerous one, Chalk Face, into the boot of the car and wedged the other one on the floor behind the driver's seat. Then he'd hoisted himself behind the steering wheel and headed off. He'd driven to a deserted place, near a stinking canal with sewage emptying into it. Parking the jeep in the thicket near by, he'd slashed the tyres and thrown the ignition key into the canal. The string wouldn't hold much longer. He'd realized Skinny Bloke would eventually break free and liberate his fellow hit man.

Albert had run back up a slip road towards a motorway café he'd spotted from the jeep. At last he'd be able to eat. Rifling through the pockets of the B Corp workers, as he called them, he'd found a key and a BIT mobile phone. But the phone was an old model not worth keeping. Plus five hundred in cash. A stroke of luck, because all he had on him were Swiss francs. He hadn't been able to pay for anything with his card since B Corp security used it to track him down in Geneva. The only valuable thing he had left was his entrance pass to B Corp HQ near Gruyères, Switzerland. But he had no intention of returning there. Apart from sometimes, in his thoughts...

He could see himself back at his desk. His team leader's desk. "The Einstein of computer games" they'd called him. Golem was going to revolutionize the world of games. It was based on a simple idea. The gamer became a small anonymous warrior whose face was masked by a helmet. There were three possible journeys. One led to the heroic fantasy of Golemia. Another offered a ticket to Golem City, a place Batman would have been proud of. And the third plunged you into the horror of Golem-Okh. At the end of each journey, the player could bring a golem to life by typing the word EMET, meaning "truth" in Hebrew.

Albert had tried out the game on all his co-workers. Each of them had, in turn, made their own golems by choosing from an infinite number of possible combinations. Albert noticed how much the gamer revealed of his or her true nature. You were free to give your golem the body of a supermodel or the murderous impulses of a psychopath. Gamers thought they were God. But at the same time, through a diabolical twist, they became slaves to the game. Golem was a nasty piece of work. Fortunately, not many people knew about it...

Albert rubbed his forehead: he had a migraine. He paid for his meal and headed back to his motel room. He needed to sleep. Sleep. Sleep.

But in his dreams he kept running. Like a madman, across Geneva. The famous water jet was in sight. Chalk Face and Skinny Bloke were hot on his heels. He just needed to get to the lake. He'd be safe in the crowd of tourists...

He woke with a start. He looked around him, dazed. He was in his motel room and the workers from B Corp weren't on his tail. Then he remembered the two trussed-up Sunday roasts he'd abandoned in the jeep, and started laughing.

He had a shower. The hot water made him feel better. He'd been panicking too much recently.

He needed to calm down and reprogram. First priority: make sure his computer was safe.

That electric blue model had been on quite a journey since Switzerland. Albert had slipped it in with a batch of computers destined for B Corp's main UK warehouse. It was meant to stay there, with the rest of the stock, until he was ready to come and retrieve it. But some idiot had got it mixed up with the Price Shrinkers stock and it had been dispatched to the "lucky winners" on the Moreland Estate. In any case, the computer seemed to enjoy escaping from him. But was this about the computer, or what was *inside* it? Even under all that hot water, Albert couldn't help shivering. What had the kid said to him? The printer had started up by itself. Which was impossible, of course.

He stepped out of the shower and stretched. He'd eaten and slept, and he was feeling good. Intelligence: 160. Character: *awkward*. Special powers: *black belt in judo*. Weapons: *knuckleduster, flick knife, Beretta*. Skills: *not a lot…*

What's Inside a Computer?

A sickening feeling in the pit of your stomach. Like when you're scared of getting blasted for a bad mark. Or being done for stealing a CD from Big B Stores. You think you know what it is. You think you know, but you don't.

Right now, Majid felt scared every time the handle turned: who was trying to get in? Scared when he had to leave the flat: who was on the other side of the door? Scared when the lift doors opened: who was going to step out? He was scared stiff. And it had been going on for nearly a week. He had to talk to somebody, and he had to get rid of the computer.

He had to get rid of this sickening feeling in the pit of his stomach.

Hugh had just finished sleeping off the sangria when Majid rang his doorbell early Saturday morning.

"Had we arranged a meeting?" asked the young English teacher. His hangover made him tetchy.

Majid went straight to the point. "My life's in danger."

More trouble on the Moreland Estate. Hugh sighed. "OK, what have you done this time?"

"The delivery men from Price Shrinkers came back last Sunday night. They wanted to take my computer off me." Trembling, Majid told Hugh about the two men bursting in. He felt like he was reliving it all.

"Unbelievable," murmured Hugh. "They'll stop at nothing."

"Wait. There's more."

Majid hadn't mentioned Albert yet. Hugh found it hard to take Albert's intervention seriously. That kind of Action Man behaviour was reserved for Gordon Freeman in Half-Life.

"He told me to hide the computer, so I thought maybe…"

Hugh saw what was coming. "You could hide it here?" he finished, pulling a face.

They both fell silent. Then Majid repeated Albert's words. "It's not an ordinary computer."

"Why don't you tell the police?" Hugh suggested.

"They'd never believe me. You hardly believe me, as it is."

"Maybe we should warn MI6? I wonder if it's some kind of industrial espionage? Your computer's one of the latest models."

"And there's something inside it," Majid added.

"Some technological breakthrough, I guess. Your computer was delivered by mistake. There are people out there who want to steal it, and others who want to get it back." The more he talked, the less scared Hugh felt. He was even beginning to feel quite excited. This was definitely a Gordon Freeman-style adventure. He made up his mind. "We'll tell your mum my computer's better than yours for learning how to spell properly."

"Are we doing a swap then?" asked Majid, relieved.

Convincing Mrs Mullins proved more difficult. She had enough problems trying to work on Hugh's computer as it was, and now he wanted to make her use an even more high-tech model. But they managed to do the swap all the same and Hugh rushed to plug in the New Generation BIT computer.

"What are you doing? Have you gone crazy?" Majid panicked. "You're not going to start it up? Albert said not to play Golem any more!"

Hugh pretended to look around for Albert. "Where is Superman then? I need a computer for my work. So..." He switched the computer on. Majid stepped back, as if the machine might explode at any moment.

"In any case," Hugh added, "Albert wasn't against using the computer. He just said not to play Golem—"

"Golemmmm," echoed around the room.

"Switch it off!" cried Majid.

Hugh almost did, but then checked himself. "Calm down. What's the big deal?"

"What if there's a bomb inside?"

Hugh shrugged. "A bomb would already have exploded."

"And what if it only explodes when you've finished the game?"

Hugh sat down in front of the computer. "Well, let's find out."

Majid paused for a split second before sitting down next to his teacher. "Phwoar!" he exclaimed when he saw Natasha on the screen. "You've made her totally fit now. What's that weapon?"

"An eraser-laser."

"How does it work?"

Hugh grabbed his mouse. *Peowww! Peowww!* Beams shot out of the weapon, triggering a series of small on-screen explosions. Blue-white sparks flashed and crackled.

"Ouch! I bet that hurts," exclaimed Majid admiringly. "And what are those flames up at the top?"

There were five of them.

"Natasha's five lives. I won them in Golemia."

Majid looked at the door, behind which he knew all the monsters were lurking. "There's only one thing for it..."

"No," protested Hugh. It was beyond his girl-golem's powers.

"Yeah, but as it is, we're stuck."

"I know."

Hugh moved the cursor around the screen. But the door was the only way out. Sighing heavily like somebody throwing down their last card, he clicked on the door.

They heard the rattling sound of a typewriter but, unlike on previous occasions, no words flashed up on the screen. Instead, two small bright squares framed the warrior and Bubble the dragon, shrinking them both and relocating them to the top of the screen. From now on they were icons the player could click on.

"The protagonist's changed," Hugh pointed out, his hand still glued to the mouse.

"The *what*?" asked Majid, who always got annoyed when Hugh talked in teacher-speak.

The door opened slowly. No monsters in sight.

"It's a different character playing now," Hugh explained. "Come on, Natasha, let's get going…"

He spoke these last words tenderly. She might be a warrior, but she was a girl too. And what a girl! Somewhere between a vamp and a lioness, with all those curves. She headed over to the open door and walked through it. The camera swivelled round. Back view of Natasha. Now face on. The wind ruffled her hair, lifting her golden fringe. There were four letters inscribed on her forehead: EMET. The truth.

"Was that what the typewriter was doing?" Hugh asked, a lump in his throat.

Natasha bore the sign of the golem in faded letters on her flesh. She was branded like a slave.

"That's disgusting," Majid said quietly.

Fortunately her hair fell back into place, hiding that shameful symbol again.

Great graphics: fields, woods and flowers. The girl-golem was on the lookout as she advanced lithely. Suddenly she saw the head of a gnome in a tree, like a knot in the wood. She could always spot her enemies, however subtle they tried to be.

"Eraser-laser!" shouted Majid.

Peowww! A laser ray blew up the gnome. Natasha carried on, as if she'd just stopped to pick a flower.

Golem's creator had programmed an interactive

sequence for the gamer to try out his or her weapon. The graphics kept changing. The countryside turned into a garden, with marble statues that sometimes sprang to life, bird baths swarming with vipers and fountains decorated with tentacles. The enemies didn't attack Natasha. They escorted her. And Hugh wiped them out with glee.

She finally arrived at a fake grotto, the kind of thing you'd find in the grounds of an old-fashioned stately home. Hugh didn't really want to go in, but the girl-golem forced her way through the murky graphics. She could see in the dark, so Calimero and Magic Berber could also make out the inside of the grotto, bathed in watery light.

"Draw near," boomed a deep voice through the loudspeakers.

Majid and Hugh were startled. They noticed a black hairy creature on a rockery throne. It was stooped but wore a crown.

"A monkey?" whispered Majid.

Hugh was breathing jerkily, his hand hovering over the mouse.

"Draw near, golem," the voice continued. "Do not be frightened. I am the Old Monkey, the master of these gardens. And now it is your turn to speak. So tell me, golem, what is your name?"

"I am … Natasha."

Hugh felt a tingle of pleasure when he heard her voice.

"Golem Natasha," the monkey went on, "truth has set you on your path. But you do not have a soul. The Master Golem alone can turn you into a real human being."

"Where can I find the Master Golem?"

"It is up to you to find out. Continue on your way and beware of the Evildoers…"

The sound suddenly went fuzzy, the picture froze and then disappeared. When Orpheus lost Eurydice for ever, he probably looked as moody as Hugh did then.

"Aargh, ma-aa-an!" groaned Majid. "Just when it was getting interesting."

That evening, Calimero realized he would have no peace until he'd visited the Master Golem to ask for Natasha's soul.

Lulu

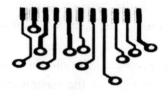

Sebastian wasn't top of the class for nothing. And thanks to his new friend's scientific knowledge, Samir had come to the conclusion that Majid's computer was the site of paranormal phenomena.

That Saturday the two boys were at Sebastian's house.

"We've got to warn Majid," said Samir.

"He already knows. Aisha said he saw some kind of ghost in the basements too."

"Yeah, but we've got to tell him about your trans-doodah…"

Samir was taking so many books off the shelves that he was starting to get on Sebastian's nerves.

In some of them you could see photos of greyish TV screens tinged with slightly darker stains. The authors declared these to be "unquestionably" noses, beards and the outlines of breasts. Basically they were dead people, in pieces, but keen to communicate. It had been proved.

"They couldn't publish it if it wasn't true," Sebastian pointed out.

Samir agreed. "But why did the monster in the basements come out of the computer?" he asked, his voice wobbling the way it did every time he mentioned the blob-shaped golem.

"It's an ectoplasm," said Sebastian, and reeled off the definition. "It's the barely visible substance of the peri-spirit or psyche belonging to those who live on the other side." The problem, according to Sebastian, was that these beings from the other side might come out of the basements and start harassing the residents of Hummingbird Tower. "You live on the first floor, don't you?" he asked casually.

Samir swallowed. The ectoplasm might not be as barely visible as all that, and it might just drop by his flat. Even though he hadn't smoothed things over with Majid following his trick in the basements, he decided he had to tell him about his computer. He had to explain the danger. Because in his flat was the only thing Samir treasured in the world, the only person he loved. His sister, Lulu.

Lulu who was six years old but looked four because of her disease. Lulu who already had more years behind her than ahead of her. Lulu who was all alone in the flat, from the time Samir left for school in the morning to when he got home in the afternoon.

Samir would have been relieved to learn the New Generation BIT computer was no longer in Hummingbird Tower. As relieved as Majid was feeling since Hugh had agreed to the swap. That afternoon, Majid decided to celebrate with a trip to Big B Stores. He wanted to buy some fluorescent farting goo. He stood deliberating in front of the stacks of little tubs. Green or yellow? He reached for a green.

Suddenly he felt himself being shoved. A kid from Moreland Estate Primary lunged at a tub of FG. "Wicked! Coconut! That's a rare one!"

Majid felt like lashing out at the kid, but instead

asked, "What? More rare than fluorescent?"

"You what? A coconut's worth at least two fluos, innit? OK, I'm off to cereals, man. Have you seen the special offer? There's, like, an FG inside every Special B cereal packet. Just regular FGs, geddit? But they're free."

Majid watched the kid head off. It was sickening. Year 6s knew more about FG than he did. He put down his fluorescent tub and made his way over to the cereals aisle. Sure enough, Special B cereal was launching its spring campaign. Printed in big letters on every box was a jingle that was impossible to miss:

Inside this packet there's a present for you:
a regular tub of farting goo!
Collect farting points too!
Ten points: one fluorescent tub
Twenty points: one scented tub

Each Special B cereal packet was worth two points. There was also a game to play: WIN THE MYSTERY TUB! Majid read the competition questions as he stood in front of the shelf: How many different kinds of farting goo are there? How many scented tubs? How many regular colours and how many fluorescent colours?

"Easy," piped up a voice next to him.

It was the brat from Year 6 again. Majid walked off, fuming. He didn't have enough money to buy a packet of cereal. In the end he went back to the toys aisle and picked up a fluorescent green tub again.

"Pssst!"

He looked round. It was Samir. Majid clenched his fists, ready for a fight. It was Samir's fault he'd been accused of jacking car radios last term.

"Yeah, I know," said Samir sheepishly, "you've still got beef with me. Look, man, I'm sorry…"

The class rebel was finally apologizing. But Majid was still angry. "Fool," he said between gritted teeth.

Samir brushed off the insult. "Drop it. I want to talk to you. We're in danger. Come on."

Majid froze with his tub of farting goo in his hand.

"I'm telling you, we're in danger. It's because of your computer. Come on…"

Majid recognized the scared look in Samir's

eyes. It matched his own. And if the two boys had seen what was happening at Hummingbird Tower at that very moment, they'd have realized they were right to be scared.

In the empty flat on the first floor, Lulu pushed back her bedclothes and looked at her deformed feet. She'd struggled to edge herself up her pillow into a sitting position. All her joints ached. She knew that one day she wouldn't even be able to sit up in bed by herself, or hug Koala, or turn the pages of her Moomin books. Much less walk.

It wasn't her fault she was ill. But, she thought to herself, it *was* her fault everything was going wrong. All the medicines she had to take were expensive. That was why there was never enough money at home, why her mum was sad and her dad drank too much. It didn't occur to Lulu that her dad drank too much because he was unemployed and her mum was sad because her husband didn't love her any more. She preferred to blame herself.

To kill time while she was waiting for Samir, she rubbed ointment into her burns. Nobody understood how she'd got them. She couldn't really explain it herself. One evening, she'd felt a force flooding through her. She thought she'd been cured. She got up, walked all the way to the window and then fell down, just as if she'd been struck by lightning. She wasn't in too much pain now. Or else she couldn't feel it. Pain was something she was used to.

Lulu had made up a little song. It was almost a prayer.

> Force, please come back to me.
> I need you.
> Force, please come and help me.
> Make me stand when I count to three.
> One, two—

Just as she reached the end of her song, the hand that was covered with ointment started crackling. Tiny bluish sparks flashed from her fingers. It didn't hurt but it felt and looked funny.

One, two, three. The Force was back.

Stand up, Lulu told herself.

She got up slowly and went over to the window. There were now bluish sparks flashing all over her body. They tickled. She glanced outside. The Force was with her, and she could go wherever she wanted. She made it as far as the kitchen, but she wasn't hungry or thirsty. What about the TV in the living room? No, she didn't feel like switching it on.

She felt like going out.

Just thinking about it made her head spin. It'd been such a long time since she'd gone outside on her own two feet. On the rare occasions when she'd left Hummingbird Tower, it had been for a trip to the hospital. And she'd been carried on a stretcher.

She reached the front door and rested her hand on the metal doorknob. She got an electric shock. She pulled her hand back sharply. How was she going to open it? Then she had a brainwave. Rubber washing-up gloves. Back again, she tried touching the knob with one finger. No shock. The gloves were perfect insulators. Now she could go outside proudly upright, even though her back was twisted, and using her own two legs, even though her feet were deformed. She didn't hurt anywhere. She felt like she was floating.

When she was out on the landing, she noticed the timer-switch for the light was broken. So was the lift. She was scared of the dark. Where was she going to go? She could feel the Force drawing her, guiding her. The stairs? Putting one foot in front of the other was one thing. But going down the stairs in the dark… Lulu was frightened the Force might abandon her along the way. What if she fell?

Reluctantly she went back into the flat. The most sensible idea was to practise walking in her bed-room. Little by little, building up her muscles which had wasted away.

There were fewer blue sparks now. Lulu sat down on her bed. But the Force hadn't left her completely.

And there was something else too. Something going on inside her head. Words. Or not even. Wordless thoughts.

Thoughts that weren't hers.

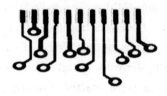

When It Gets Out

Calimero couldn't take any more. He was all out, dead beat, spent. He'd never played such an exhausting game.

The Evildoers were everywhere. They wanted to turn Natasha into one of them: a hideous, cackling beast. Each step on the path leading to the Master Golem was a trap. As soon as Hugh relaxed, an Evildoer attacked Natasha and inflicted some kind of deformity on her, like an iron hand, or blonde curls that were actually vipers. He had to win back a hand made of flesh and blood, or a plait of real hair. And in order to do that, he had to spend some gold, use the first-aid kit, lose a life, get the little warrior or the dragon to help him. It was a non-stop battle. And it was hot, unusually hot for the beginning of May. Hugh's brain was boiling over. His sweat-soaked shirt stuck to his skin and he couldn't tear his shining eyes from the screen. But he was smiling. He'd survived the first round.

Natasha was safe for the time being in a miniature Eden, a delicate rose garden where fountains flowed. Her escort was Bubble the dragon. But he was a miniature dragon now, spitting miniature flames. Calimero had sent the warrior away, and kept this scaled-down version of Bubble as Natasha's companion.

"Dinner's ready!" Mrs Mullins called out from the other side of the study door.

Hugh stretched, blew his girl-golem a kiss and saved the game.

"Hugh, it's getting cold!"

"I'm not, though," the young man whispered, getting up slowly.

He sat down absent-mindedly at the table.

"Did you have a lot of marking to do?" his mother asked sympathetically.

"Mmm? Yeah, loads!" Hugh hadn't even started.

"One of your students called, but I didn't want to disturb you. He said his name was Majid."

"What did he want?"

"I'm not sure, really. It was to do with your computer. He's got to give a presentation. Something about making the right connection? It's for his IT class, I think…"

Intrigued, Hugh shook his head. More trouble.

"This heat is something else," added Mrs Mullins.

Night fell over Moreland Town, as stifling as a thick blanket you can't shrug off. In the basements of Hummingbird Tower, behind door 401, Sebastian's ectoplasm could detect the storm coming long before the first rumbles were heard. The estate looked almost beautiful lit up by flashes of lightning, but there was nobody around to appreciate it. At half past midnight, everybody was asleep.

In the heart of the old town, not far from the grey concrete towers of the Moreland Estate, a greenish light was reflected in a window. It was the faint glow not of a lamp but of a computer. In the darkness of the room, against the grey background of the screen saver, a cube kept rotating as it turned into a flower and back again. It was called a 3D flowering box. Hugh had forgotten to switch off his computer before staggering from his study to his bed.

A power surge disturbed it. The 3D box vanished. More flowers appeared, less computerized this time. They were the flowers in the rose garden. And Natasha stood there among the roses, stock-still. At her feet, shrunk to the size of a family pet, Bubble the dragon looked harmless enough.

All that was missing in this picture was life.

The thunderstorm swooped down on the suburb with a great crash. Lights flickered. There was a short surge of electricity down the wires. Light bulbs popped, plastic sizzled. In the furthest corner of its basement lot, the monster sparked. And on the screen, Natasha aimed her eraser-laser at the swivel chair. Her gaze seemed to pierce the glass. Was her enemy on the other side?

A white rectangle appeared around the girl-golem. A second, smaller one framed the dragon. Each rectangle was made up of a grid pattern. The light went from white to red before becoming so dazzling that the rose garden was plunged into shadow. A single beam shone from the centre of each rectangle, like a laser. The criss-crossed pictures were projected so that they floated for a moment in the messy study. One by one, the lines were erased, like prison bars falling away.

Natasha had taken on a third dimension.

She was in the real world.

She opened her eyes wide. Where was the rose garden? She turned round, her eraser-laser ready for action, and picked her way carefully, keeping low, all her senses alert. Bubble's scaly back wound in and out between her legs.

Suddenly a girl with blonde hair and green eyes appeared in front of her. Natasha's warrior instinct made her press the trigger, firing a lethal beam of pure energy. She hit the woman on the chest, making a black mark. But the stranger didn't falter. It was just a moving image on a giant screen. A screen with a golden frame. Natasha opened her mouth. The other woman opened hers. Natasha lifted her arm. The other woman lifted hers. Natasha brushed her fringe back. And on the unknown woman's forehead she saw four letters inscribed: TᴱMᴱ.

A vivid flash of lightning filled the study. Natasha looked around. She detected the presence of hostile objects in front of the books on one of the shelves, and on a black CD player. She crouched down in combat position and fired another beam. Again and again she pressed the trigger before pausing, disconcerted. Her powers weren't so effective on this side of the screen. She wanted to destroy the objects, but all she could do was make small dark stains, thin wisps of smoke wafting up from them. The multicoloured tubs of farting goo bothered her: they bore the evil B Corp logo. She had caused similar damage to a plastic box where the same logo was followed by an enigmatic message: BIG B RECORDS: PUFF Z SNIDDY.

After the lightning came the thunder.

"Master!" Natasha called. "What is my mission?" No sound came out of her mouth. But she could hear her voice. She turned to face the computer, and saw the path between the rose bushes which she should never have left.

"Master?" Her voice was coming from the loudspeakers on either side of the screen. And, again, the letters BIT on all the different computer parts seemed to bother her. "Master! Master? They are here! They are everywhere! What is my mission?"

A Big B Stores plastic bag twitched on the floor. Natasha saw a tiny hole appear in it, then get bigger. The plastic had started to melt around Bubble's muzzle. He felt surrounded by the enemy too, and shuffled across the room, still cocooned in the bag, making ridiculous squeaking noises.

Suddenly she noticed the flowers on the table. Mrs Mullins liked roses, and put vases of them all round the flat. Natasha was fascinated. She moved closer. They were enticing and dangerous at the same time. She couldn't help stretching out her hand. Her fingers touched the top of the vase and *went through* the cold transparent glass.

"Master! What is it?"

No reply. The water danced inside the vase. The computer snored loudly and suddenly another beam of light was projected from it. It ensnared Natasha in the grid pattern again, making her lose her third dimension, and in one short in-breath it tore her away from the deadly trap.

Then the beam shot out a second time, in search of the little dragon.

Outside, the sky was packed with fat black clouds. There was another flash of lightning. Across town, the monster in basement lot 401 let out a hungry roar. More light bulbs popped, more plastic sizzled. Just as the beam of light was about to snatch up Bubble, the screen blinked. Another surge of electricity. The beam disappeared.

Bubble let out a terrified whimper. He ran towards the glowing screen. He jumped. He flapped his wings. He took off. He clawed in vain at the smooth surface of the glass. His burning mouth was biting on thin air. He fell back down again.

At that very moment, in the adjoining room, Hugh sat up in bed.

"Huh? What?"

Bubble dived under the desk. With every puff, a tiny flame singed a hole in the carpet.

"Wow, what a dream!" Hugh mumbled, rubbing his face. Half asleep, he picked up his glass of water from the bedside table. It must be the thunder that woke me, he told himself. The dream was still very clear in his mind. There'd been a woman in his study. A woman talking to him. A woman calling him.

"*Master!*"

He choked and spluttered. *Master!* For a moment, he felt like he was back at primary school. Except that nobody called their teacher master any more. The kids had plenty of other names for him. As for what the women teachers called him...

"Thugh," he whispered. "They call me Thugh."

Why was he thinking about Nadia? Had he dreamt about her? What was going on? *Master! Master!* The voice was echoing in his ears, like a cry for help. Tomorrow at school, he'd ask the science teacher if she'd slept well. No, on second thoughts, maybe not. She'd only get ideas.

Just then he noticed a faint glow filtering under his study door. His computer must still be on. He got up to turn it off. On the screen a 3D flowering box was rotating. He was wide awake now, and thinking about making a quick trip to Golemia. But he decided against it. Instead he stroked the mouse. Natasha was waiting for him behind the screen saver. Hugh felt he was drowning in her green gaze. That voice was still there, inside his head.

"*Master! What* is it?"

What are you so afraid of, Natasha? Hugh wondered. His hand tightened on the mouse. Did she want to tell him something? Tell him not to leave her. Not to…

He switched off the computer. He stood for a minute or two in front of the dark screen. Something wasn't right. Natasha had changed. She was slipping away from him.

When he finally turned his back on the computer, it struck him that she'd got rid of Bubble. He hadn't seen the little dragon next to her. He paused at his study door, and screwed up his nose. What was that burning smell? He shrugged. It must be because of the storm, he decided. Or something to do with the ozone layer…

Back in his bed he was relieved to find he felt sleepy again.

Under the desk, Bubble puffed another hole…

Genetically Modified

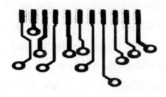

Hugh found his mother down on all fours in his study, peering under the chest of drawers.

"What's going on? Are you doing your yoga in here now?"

"Don't you think there's a funny smell? There's something under here. Something that makes holes."

Hugh made a half-hearted attempt to bend down, but didn't get far enough to see what Mrs Mullins was pointing at.

"I can't bear mice," she declared as she stood up.

"Well, if that's what it is, they must be genetically modified mice. The carpet-munching variety."

"If this room was cleaned more often... I mean,

you could at least air the place occasionally. Now, will you look at that!" His mother was pointing at a tub of farting goo on a shelf. A small black hole had punctured the green plastic.

"Help!" said Hugh. "Flying mice!"

"This study has got as many holes in it as a piece of Gruyère cheese. I'll pop round to Big B Stores. They've got a whole shelf of pest-control products."

Hugh watched his mother put the tub of farting goo in her pocket.

"We'll have to throw it out," she said. "D'you want me to get you another one the same colour?"

"Do they sell them with the pest-control products? It wouldn't surprise me. Maybe they've got—" Hugh broke off. He'd nearly asked his mother to bring him the scented kind.

This was getting seriously out of hand.

Mrs Mullins went off with the green tub. Hugh still had the red tub, the blue tub and the pink tub. A fluorescent yellow and a fluorescent mauve. It was hard to get hold of fluorescent mauves. The situation was out of control at school. Ever since the head had decided to ban FG on school premises, there had been a flourishing black market. Kids who were ahead of the game were making money left, right and centre. It was all the students talked about in the playground. News and rumours spread faster than the farting goo itself. How much was a fluorescent purple and orange striped one worth? Did a banana/strawberry scented combo really exist? Was it true you could win a Twingo car by sending the lids of the complete FG collection back to the manufacturer? According to some sources, there were sixty-three different types.

Hugh sat down in front of his computer and, without knowing why, drew up a geek-style list:

- one colour (regular, like it says on the lid): boring apart from orange and brown
- two colours: fairly common
- fluorescent: fairly common
- stripy fluorescent: rare
- musical: rare (never seen one – heard one, I mean)
- scented: coconut, lemon (sought after); wild pine forest, violet, mint (very rare)
- scented combo (very, very rare – may just be a myth)

It was a rough summary of what he'd learnt from whisperings in the corridors and playground. But there was one kind missing. He didn't know what to call it. Tinted? Its dye came off on your hands. People said you could wash it off with soap. But that wasn't the problem. There were strange rumours going around that the dye contained a hallucinogenic substance. A drug. He'd even seen something about it in the newspapers. There were weird stories of kids going crazy, describing nightmare visions. Hugh shrugged. He'd already heard plenty of tales like that during his short teaching career. All he knew for sure was he didn't have any green farting goo now. His mother had swiped his tub.

Suddenly an alarming thought struck him: Mrs Mullins had been wanting a new Twingo for a long time. Some people would stop at nothing to get their hands on FG.

Lulu felt abandoned. Like she often did. Like she always did. Samir was hanging around the estate instead of coming straight back home. She understood. She forgave him. She knew that reading

Moomin books to his little sister wasn't very exciting. Samir was out with his crew. She had no idea what they got up to. Her brother never talked about his friends. Lulu didn't have any friends. She'd never had any. It was something she'd got used to. Like being ill. Like being in pain.

She looked at her hands. The blue flames had disappeared. The Force wasn't so strong now. But she didn't hurt. She decided to get up and practise walking, while she still had some energy left. All the way round the bed. Over to the window. Three more steps.

She walked out of her bedroom and made her way down the hall cluttered with brooms and boxes of washing powder. She reached the door. She paused. Then she took the bunch of keys hanging from the hook by the door.

The bare light bulbs in the corridor were flickering in a spooky kind of way. A few floors up, somebody was cussing at the lift. It was out of order again. In any case, she wouldn't dare use it on her own. The staircase. The steps.

Amazed at how bold she was feeling, Lulu started going down, her hand gripping the cold stair rail. One step. Two steps. She counted twenty-six before she reached the ground floor. She had only been through this grey entrance hall on a stretcher, or sometimes in her dad's arms. She was heading outside, towards the light and the sun, but that wasn't what she wanted. Not today. She wanted to go down further.

She carried on. There were the big green dustbins on the right, and there were the basements on the left. She pushed open the heavy wooden door. The timer-switch was crackling: the lights might go off at any second. But Lulu wasn't frightened any more. She trotted along the underground passages, without knowing where she was going. Trusting in the Force, she let herself be led. The shadow of her tiny frame brushed over Prosper the ghost.

At the end of a long shadowy tunnel, a faint bluish light was throbbing. Lulu froze as an electric tingling spread over her whole body. She looked at her hands. Blue sparks were flashing all over her translucent skin, and her heart started beating faster. The Force was right there.

She carried on fearlessly. There were two old crates at the entrance to lot 401. She sat down, enveloped in little blue flames. "Hello," she said, "I'm Lulu."

The shapeless thing crackled. Like the sparklers Samir had stuck on her last birthday cake.

"Which Moomin are you?" she asked.

The creature made a peculiar noise.

"Is your mouth stitched up? You can't talk? Don't worry."

The monster shuffled closer. It was hunched over and looked clumsy and shy.

"No, you're not a Moomin. Well, it doesn't matter."

A heartbreaking groan answered her.

"Don't be sad. Moomins aren't very smart, you know. But you..." Lulu gazed at that ghastly head with its lifeless eyes hovering in front of her. "You're like me, you haven't been very lucky. Maybe we should try and mend you."

The pale face with its unfathomable hollows looked attentive. The monster was listening to her.

"You've got the Force. I couldn't walk before, d'you remember? It's all thanks to you. I can walk now because of you. I've come to say thank you."

The monster unhunched itself. It got a bit

closer and then hunched itself up again, as if it didn't want its bulk to scare the little girl. Carefully she held out a finger and touched it. A great electric whirlwind instantly wrapped itself around them, bringing them together. Lulu could feel her hair standing on end, as if there was a vacuum cleaner above her head. It made her laugh.

"You're tickling me," she complained happily. She stood up and took the creature's two big paws in her tiny hands. She felt a funny, cold, prickly sensation, like when the doctor wiped cotton wool soaked in ethanol over her skin. But the doctor didn't give off sparks. And he didn't make her feel like this.

Lulu wanted to dance and twirl and jump. "The Force is with me!"

The monster let itself be dragged into the dance. It grunted as it waddled about, as comic and clumsy as a grizzly bear. It looked as excited as Lulu, and maybe just as happy too.

"D'you want to be my friend?" Lulu asked.

The answer was in the emptiness of its eyes, the hole of its mouth.

"I don't know if Samir would be very pleased. We'd better not say anything, OK?"

The monster pulled back and the whirlwind stopped. Lulu was breathing heavily. "My head's spinning," she gasped, sitting back down on a crate. The monster collapsed next to her. "It's annoying having a friend who hasn't got a name. What am I going to do if I need to call you?"

The monster grunted again, its head tilted to one side.

"We'll have to think of one," she decided. "I've got to go now. Before Samir gets back. I'll come and visit you again tomorrow, when there's nobody at home."

She waggled a finger authoritatively at her new friend. "Wait a bit before you start eating any more electricity. I don't want to climb back up in the dark, OK?"

How did Lulu know the power cuts in Hummingbird Tower were linked to the monster? Was it something she'd guessed? Or had it told her, via those wordless thoughts that crept into her mind?

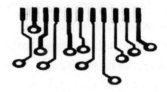

Transcommunication

Albert was kicking himself. To think he'd had that computer in his grasp and passed up the chance to get it back. A week or so ago, his main concern had been to get the B Corp workers away from Majid. He'd acted in the heat of the moment, and there'd been no time to think. He'd tried to catch the kid at home early this morning, but nobody had been in. So this afternoon he decided to go to school, which was something he hadn't done for a few years.

Half past one. Silence. Weren't the kids supposed to be kicking a football around after lunch? The car park was almost empty. Probably because the teachers couldn't afford to run a car in this dump of a suburb. He spotted something that resembled a prison officer's lookout, but was presumably the caretaker's office. There was a gate to the right. Albert didn't have his high-jumper's legs any more, but he rested his hand on it and reckoned it was within his range.

The concrete area behind the hedge was presumably the playground. Not a soul in sight. The bell must have gone. Did they still use bells? Five hundred students? Eight hundred? Thirty classes? Fifty? He was in no mood to check them out, one by one. Why had he avoided the caretaker? He could've asked him where to find Majid Badach. Slipped him something. Money gets tongues talking.

Then he noticed somebody, a young woman, crossing the playground. He ran towards her, waving. "Miss! Hey!"

She was blonde. And cute. Correction: *very* cute. She shot him a suspicious look, taking in his stubble and crumpled suit.

"Have you come about the toilets?" she enquired.

"Not my speciality."

"Weally? What are you doing here, then?"

"I need some information," said Albert. Then, unable to resist returning the compliment, he added, "Are you the caretaker?"

The pretty blonde woman gave a start. "Excuse me, but do I look like..." She broke off and ran a hand through her hair, as if suddenly having doubts. If she'd had a mirror, she'd have checked her make-up. "How did you get in?"

"The gate's not very high. Listen, I'm looking for a student. Majid."

The woman looked daggers at him. "There's no weason for you to be in this school. Are you a parent? No. Then please leave immediately." She caught her breath and added, "Mathid? Mathid Badach?"

Albert tried a seductive smile. "If you could just tell me what class he's in. It's very important."

Her face flushed with a mixture of surprise and suspicion. "The students aren't here," she revealed. "It's extwa-cuwicular activities afternoon."

Albert burst out laughing. "And what's your ... extwa-cuwicular activity?"

Nadia gave him a cold stare. She was past the

age of being teased about her speech impediment. "I make chemical pweparations. If you're interested, come to the lab with me." She waited for a big grin to break across Albert's face before adding, "I've got enough acid to dissolve every molecule of your body."

With that parting remark she turned and headed off briskly. Back in the lab, in front of her flasks and test tubes, Nadia felt like bursting into tears. Men!

While Albert was having no luck at Moreland School, Majid and Samir had arrived in front of the semi-detached house where Sebastian lived.

"Hey," said Majid, "he's got a garden. Weird! You open your bedroom window and see flowers."

"There's nuff books inside," Samir confided. "No wonder he's top in everything. He's got it all in there – dictionaries, encyclopedias, the works."

Sebastian didn't share their enthusiasm. "They're all boring around here," he told them, taking his classmates up to his room. "They're all old ladies and dogs."

On the stairs, Majid admired some strange

paintings on the walls that weren't of anything in particular. Just splashes of colour. It was abstract art, Sebastian explained. Useful, thought Majid, if you couldn't draw. He'd try it out next time he didn't know how to spell something. A splash of ink. An abstract word.

Modern art didn't do a lot for Samir, but the equipment lined up on the bedroom carpet produced a more favourable response. Sebastian stood in the way, deliberately blocking his access.

"This gear's worth loads of money, all right? So, respect. Handle it with a lot of care." Like any top student about to make a presentation, he did a quick recap. "Right, I've got the spotlights, the camcorder, the webcam… OK, let's pack them up!" His parents were keen rock climbers, so there were plenty of rucksacks to go round. "Whoops!" he said suddenly. "I nearly forgot the wall."

"No problem," Samir said, and mimed lifting one up.

Sebastian ignored him. "For the projection. I hope there's a white wall at Mr Mullins's. In fact," he added, turning to Majid, "what exactly did you say to him?"

"That we were going to talk to dead people on TV."

Sebastian's eyes bulged. "And ... he's all right about that?"

"Kind of."

Samir frowned. How was all this going to get rid of the monster or ectoplasm or whatever it was?

Fully loaded up, the three boys headed off and joined the scrum to catch the bus. There was a bus stop just outside the red-brick apartment building where their teacher lived.

Hugh welcomed them with a tense smile. He hadn't understood a word of Majid's explanation. He looked at the backpacks dumped in the hall.

"So," he said to Sebastian, "what's all this gear for?"

"A scientific experiment, sir."

"Scientific as in: 'Spirit, knock three times if you're not there'?"

"Watch it, sir," Samir interrupted. "That stuff's worth nuff dollars. There's a camcorder and everything. So no messing."

"OK, but let's get on with it. I don't want my mother walking in mid-seance. She's a materialist." When he saw his students looking confused, he added, "She doesn't believe in spirits."

According to Hugh, all his study walls were white. But you had to take his word for it, because they were hidden behind shelf after shelf of books. They decided to hang a sheet in front of the books. Hugh followed Sebastian's hesitant instructions and plugged in the different bits of equipment. The wires got knotted on the carpet, but finally they were all connected up to the computer.

"The idea's to have it on a loop," Sebastian explained. "We'll use the camcorder to film the sheet lit by the spotlights. The webcam films the computer screen. That way, we get a white picture full of static interference. We turn the video on, and it records the picture—"

"Hold on," said Hugh. "The camcorder plugged into the computer films the sheet, and the webcam films the screen where we see the sheet. Am I right?"

"Er ... yes."

"And then you use the video to record this

show-stopper? To get a close-up of the white with its static interference?"

"Yep."

Hugh scratched his head as if, for once, he was the one who didn't know the answer. "And what d'you get on your tape, apart from white and interference?"

"Transcommunication," said Sebastian firmly.

"How on earth d'you get that?"

"Because ... er ... because we've called on the spirits. They've got into the video system. And by decoding the frequency, we'll find out what their message is."

"Exactly!" agreed Samir.

"I don't get it," Majid admitted.

Samir sighed loudly. "The sheet. There's always a ghost under the sheet."

"OK, let's get started." Hugh inserted a blank tape into the video recorder.

"I'll draw the curtains," said Sebastian. "We need it to be dark. Does anybody know a prayer?"

Worried silence.

"Never mind. Would you mind turning on the spotlights, sir?"

In the murky gloom of the study, splashes of colour merged on the big crumpled sheet.

"The thing about calling up dead people is you have to do it with respect. And you have to choose who you want to call up."

"D'you mean the monster?" said Majid. "But it hasn't got a name."

"Hold on a minute. What monster?" asked Hugh. He was genuinely starting to worry about his students' mental well-being.

"You know, sir," said Samir. "The monster in the basements. Wakey-wakey. That's what we're here for."

"The monster in the basements," repeated Hugh.

The boys looked at one another. It occurred to them that they'd never told a grown-up about the monster.

"There's a monster in the basements of Hummingbird Tower," said Sebastian very quietly.

"Of course there is," answered Hugh wearily. "So?"

Sebastian lost his nerve and Samir carried on.

"Yeah, so we've got to transcommunicate with

it to find out … to find out…"

"We can't leave a soul in pain to wander the basements of Hummingbird Tower!" Sebastian pleaded.

"No, of course not," Hugh pretended to agree.

"Especially when it's a dangerous monster," said Samir. "We've got to send it back there … to its astral doodah. You know. Like, its base."

"Absolutely. The astral base it is!" said Hugh, folding his arms like he was in class, waiting to see how his students would tackle an assignment.

"Shh! It's filming," said Sebastian.

The three boys were sitting on the floor. Hugh joined them, completing the circle. Depending on where they were positioned, they were staring at either the sheet where the spotlights projected vivid splashes of blue and red, or the computer screen covered in electronic snow, across which a shadow without a face wandered every now and then.

"What's that?" whispered Majid.

"It looks a bit like a copy of the game," Hugh answered. "Gol—"

"Shh!" ordered Sebastian.

Samir was getting fidgety. "Is your techno party going to last long?" he asked anxiously.

"We haven't even started yet!" said Sebastian. "Concentrate, OK? Right, I'm ready." He took a deep breath and held out his arms, palms up. "Spirit lost at the physical level, tortured soul, you who wander through the basements of Hummingbird Tower, speak to us so we may come to your rescue."

Hugh listened in stunned silence. This session was proving to be a revelation: boys who were top of the class could also be total basket cases.

Sebastian paused. The seconds ticked by, interrupted only by whirring noises from the equipment: the computer, the tape turning in the video recorder. Then he carried on.

"Spirit of Hummingbird Tower, we are focusing our thoughts and prayers so that you may reach the astral plane at last. Tell us what your pain is, so we may calm and comfort you, and your tortured soul may come to rest. Er... Amen."

On the screen the snow was falling more thickly now. The spotlights were flashing. Hugh felt like an idiot. Staring at dots of light and splashes of colour with a bunch of kids who'd been watching too much TV. Sebastian was off again, calling on his spirit of Hummingbird Tower. He'd always seemed such a well-balanced kid in class, Hugh mused, but Samir was turning out to be altogether more normal.

A pot-bellied ghost crossed the computer screen.

"Is that it?"

"D'you reckon?"

Hugh knew exactly what it was. The golem was hanging around, waiting just like *he* was for this crackpot seance to finish. Right, he thought. Two more minutes and I'm blowing the whistle for break.

Samir started clicking his fingers, in time to the dance of the bright dots. Majid was whistling quietly. Sebastian didn't move. His eyes were wide open and he was concentrating hard. From the video counter, Hugh could see that this farce had been going on for seven minutes and forty-six seconds. Forty-seven ... forty-eight...

"Whoooo! Whoooo!" burst out Samir.

Majid tried to suppress a laugh that ended up coming out of his nostrils in a disgusting snort.

Sebastian lashed out. Samir retreated, knocking his shoulder on the chest of drawers. "Phew-ee!" he exclaimed melodramatically.

"It's not me." Sebastian turned red.

"I mean it, it's like a burning smell," said Samir, getting ready to dodge another kick.

Hugh sniffed and also noticed a smell that was becoming familiar. A smell of—

A monstrous howl assaulted his ears. He jumped to his feet and rushed to turn on his desk light. Samir was writhing about in agony on the floor.

"My hand! My hand!"

"Calm down, Samir!" Hugh caught hold of his student's arm. "Don't move. That's it." Quickly he removed the mousetrap that had snapped shut on Samir's finger. But the kid carried on howling like somebody possessed.

"You'll be fine," Hugh reassured him. "Go and run some cold water over it. I'm sorry. My mother's scared of mice."

"My hand! It really hurts! Owww…"

"Come on, Samir, it's not as bad as—" Hugh broke off, horrified. On the back of Samir's hand, distinct from the reddening bruise made by the trap, was a nasty black mark. A burn.

It was just like the one on the carpet. And on the tub of farting goo.

"I don't understand," he stammered. "There's something going on here. Things—"

"What's going on here? What things?"

Hugh gave a start. He could see his mother's silhouette framed in the doorway. "Mum…"

"You could have told me you were planning a get-together. What do you call them these days? Farting goo parties?"

"Great, it's ruined now," Sebastian complained.

"It hurts!" moaned Samir.

Mrs Mullins walked over to the window and threw open the curtains. "What's ruined? And what hurts? What have you done to him? Oi, that's my sheet!"

Hugh tried to make his head disappear into his neck. He suddenly felt like he was twelve years old again, and he'd got caught making stink bombs with the neighbour's kids.

"Come with me," Mrs Mullins ordered Samir, frogmarching him to the bathroom.

Hugh brought the transcommunication seance

to an end. Stop! Enough! Off! Without saying a word, Sebastian and Majid helped him unplug the equipment and fold the sheet. When Mrs Mullins came back with Samir, he was wearing a bandage that went from his wrist to the tip of his middle finger.

"You like being wrapped up like a mummy, don't you?" Sebastian teased him.

Mrs Mullins confronted her son. "I'm not sure I understand what this boy's been telling me. Have you been talking to the dead?"

Majid took a step forward, as if to protect a friend who'd been unfairly accused. "We'll tidy everything up, Mrs Mullins," he said very politely. "We just wanted to do a bit of transcommunication with … Mr Mullins."

"I beg your pardon!" she exclaimed icily. "How dare you!"

Hugh felt acutely embarrassed as he watched his mother's face seize up with emotion. He knew only too well that, as far as she was concerned, there was only one Mr Mullins. Her late husband. His father. "Mum," he muttered, "it's not what you're thinking."

"So who *are* you communicating with? And why are you doing it in my home? Samir told me about a tape. Show me. I want to see it."

Reluctantly Hugh did as he was told. He pressed the rewind button and switched to the video channel. The TV screen was filled with waves and dots. "There you go," he said. "White. Static interference. It goes on like that for quarter of an hour."

Behind him, Samir was still cradling his injured hand. Meanwhile, Sebastian was scrutinizing the image on the screen, as if expecting the infamous monster of Hummingbird Tower to pop up at any moment. From time to time, a fleeting shape seemed to appear. A vague human outline, a hazy, undefined landscape. Then it was swept away, erased by a new wave of black and white dots.

"It almost looks like…" whispered Majid.

"A face," suggested Sebastian.

"It's nothing," declared Hugh. "Nothing at all."

Mrs Mullins grabbed the remote control. "I want to see that again," she said decisively.

Hugh shrugged. He had no doubt that these phenomena were images from Golem trying to install themselves. Images as blurred as when you watch a programme without plugging in the TV aerial.

"I'm going to play that section again in slow motion," his mother announced. "Maybe it'll be clearer."

For Majid, it *was* clearer. "It's Golem!" he shouted. "The bit with the caves and the Old Monkey."

"Yes," Hugh agreed wearily, "I know."

"And look! There are some letters," Majid insisted. "Words with letters in them." *Abstract words*, he nearly added.

"Yes," said Hugh dully. "Words with letters in them."

"A B and an R!" shouted Sebastian triumphantly.

"So?" Hugh's lack of excitement was evident.

"Bra!" said Samir, who wasn't big on spelling.

"Brand, more like," Majid corrected him.

"I can't see an N or a D," murmured Mrs Mullins doubtfully.

"It's a message," crowed Sebastian. "I'm sure it's a message from the other side."

"And what scintillating message has the other side got for us?" growled Hugh.

"Farting bra!" tried Samir.

The boys burst out laughing.

"Buy!" said Hugh, peering at the screen. "Buy Big… Oh no!"

"What, sir?"

"Buy Big Brand *farting goo*," Hugh concluded in a worried voice. "That's the message from beyond."

They fell silent as they were all struck by the same sad realization: in a world ruled by market forces, even the spirits were business-minded.

Majid and Samir walked slowly back to Hummingbird Tower, their hands in their pockets. Hugh had offered to drive Sebastian and his equipment back to his house. Glad of a chance to air the flat, his mother had held out the keys to her old Twingo. According to her, there were bad vibes around the place.

Hugh parked in front of Sebastian's house. Just as his student was about to get out, he asked, "By the way, Sebastian, have you heard about a kind of farting goo that stains?"

Sebastian looked surprised. "Er, yes. It's like those lollipops that dye your tongue different colours. Why? Are you collecting it?"

"I'm being serious, Sebastian. Have you played with it, you three? Samir, Majid and you."

"It's for losers, sir. I'm not into that kind of thing."

"What about your friends?" Hugh pressed him.

"I don't know. Why are you asking? I don't believe spirits can sell farting goo."

"I don't think they can either."

"So what do you think?"

Hugh shrugged. "I'm asking a few questions, that's all. I don't think it's normal that you boys should be convinced you've found a monster in the basements."

"What's that got to do with FG?"

"There are rumours going around, Sebastian. About FG. The kind that stains. They're saying there are hallucinogenic substances in the food dyes. Do you see what I'm getting at?"

"Maybe," said Sebastian, grabbing hold of his equipment. He put the backpacks down by the garden fence. "If you don't believe us, why don't you go and see for yourself?"

"That's exactly what I plan to do."

"Be careful. Take some holy water with you.

Don't forget. Holy water!"

Hugh watched Sebastian disappear inside his house. There was *definitely* a screw loose in that boy's head.

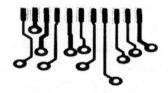

Anybody for a Drink?

When Samir and Majid got back to Hummingbird Tower, one of them couldn't find somebody who was meant to be there, and the other found somebody who wasn't.

The boys went their separate ways on the first floor.

"Good luck with the stairs," said Samir at the door to his flat, putting his key in the lock. For a change, there was something wrong with the lift, so Majid still had eleven floors to climb. Samir walked into the tiny, cluttered hallway. "It's me!" he called out.

No answer. Lulu must be asleep. He stuck his

head round her bedroom door to check his kid
sister was tucked up snugly.

Koala was sleeping all alone, in the middle of
the pillow.

"Lulu! Lulu!"

Samir knew he was shouting himself hoarse for
nothing. The only place Lulu could be was bed.
And the biggest adventure likely to happen to her
was falling out of it. He raced round the other
rooms, just in case she'd managed to crawl somewhere. Then he checked to see if her bedroom
window was closed, just in case...

"Lulu! Lulu!" he groaned.

He rushed out of the flat, pausing for a second
on the main landing, heart thumping. He could
hear Majid bravely working his way up, floor by
floor. He cast his mind back to what his classmate
had said about those strange men hanging around
the Moreland Estate. They'd tried to get his computer back off him. Majid hadn't told him much,
but he had said the men would stop at nothing.
Even kidnapping a disabled little girl? Samir wondered, terror-stricken. But why would they do that?

He knew why. He didn't have a computer, but

he'd got something else. The New Generation BIT mobile phone he'd taken from the corpse in the basements of Hummingbird Tower. Weirdly it was still charged up.

Pride stopped him running up to the twelfth floor to pour out his worries to Majid. Instead, he went back down to the main entrance hall. Just as he was heading outside, he noticed something on the ground, near the big green dustbins. He went over and found the mug Lulu always drank from. She held it by both handles and sucked from it like a baby. Samir could see it was still half full of water. And when he looked around, he noticed that the door to the basements was ajar.

Horrible images crept into his head.

Since his conversation with Sebastian, he had been worried about the ectoplasm escaping from its lair to pay the residents of Hummingbird Tower a visit. Starting with those on the first floor.

But maybe the reality was even worse.

Maybe the monster had decided to lure its victims down to the basements. Starting with…

"Lulu!" he screamed, flinging wide the heavy wooden door.

There was a cloud of smoke floating in the stairwell between the eleventh and twelfth floors. Majid froze in the gloom, alarmed. He recognized the strange phenomenon Aisha had told him about. The timer-switch for the light had just clicked off again. As he went to press the button, a brighter glow caught his eye. It was flickering just above him in the stairwell, like a firefly.

"Are you going to press it, then?"

Albert was sitting on a step, a pile of cigarette butts at his feet. "Does that lift ever work?"

"At least the lights aren't brucked," said Majid, when he'd recovered from the shock.

Albert snorted. "Two minutes forty-three seconds that timer-switch lasts. I'm fed up with getting up for it." He drew himself up to his full height as Majid squeezed past, giving him a frightened look. "You're not an easy guy to get hold of," said Albert, following him along the landing. "You're never at home, never at school... Where d'you hang out?"

"I go to school," Majid defended himself. "But today's activities afternoon."

Albert sniggered. "Yeah, so I've been told. By one of your teachers. A blonde number. You know her?"

Majid shrugged as he pretended to search for his key.

"You know who I mean?" Albert persisted. "Pretty. 'Mathid? Are you looking for Mathid?'"

Majid couldn't help laughing. "That's my science teacher, Miss Martin. Nadia, I think she's called."

"Nadia," Albert echoed approvingly. "Nice name. She's very cute, your teacher. But a bit uptight, maybe?"

Majid said nothing. He wasn't sure what Albert meant by uptight.

But Albert wouldn't let the subject drop. He leant casually against the wall. "I think I messed up with her. Tell me, Majid, d'you think I've got a chance with a woman like that?"

"No way!" Majid blushed. "For one thing, she's—"

"Married?" Albert guessed, pretending to be heartbroken.

"No, but..." Majid nearly said, "She's with Mr

Mullins." But it wouldn't have been true. So instead he said, "She fancies another teacher."

Albert sighed and lit yet another cigarette. Majid was thinking he'd have to fetch the dustpan and brush, or the caretaker would kick up a fuss.

"What about you? What d'you make of her?"

As far as Majid was concerned, Nadia was just his science teacher. End of story. But Albert was talking to him man to man, and he wanted to rise to the challenge. "Too … uptight," he agreed. "Anyway, I don't like blondes."

They heard footsteps a few floors down, echoing up the concrete stairwell.

"You found your key yet?" said Albert suddenly.

Majid dug out the gold-coloured key. He was about to put it in the lock when, recognizing the breathing of the person who'd just reached the twelfth floor, he turned round. There was Aisha with her tongue hanging out, lugging shopping bags full of fizzy drinks and cereal boxes.

She took a frightened step back when she saw the stranger on the landing. "Hi," she said to Majid, avoiding Albert's gaze.

"All right?"

"I'm OK. The lift's out of order."

"Yeah, it's brucked innit."

It was hopeless. Majid could never find anything interesting to say to Aisha.

She glanced at Albert. He was fit! He looked like he'd just stepped off a film set. "See you tomorrow," she said, disappearing into her flat.

Albert was still leaning against the wall. He smirked. "So you prefer brunettes, hey?"

Majid could feel himself flushing to the roots of his hair. He turned the key. He knew the flat was empty because Emmay had gone to visit her fifth son Moussa for the day. He went in and Albert followed, uninvited. It didn't take him a second to size up the situation.

"Don't tell me you haven't got the computer any more?" he exclaimed, staring at the old model which now had pride of place on the dining table.

"Well, you told me to hide it."

"But where is it?"

Majid clammed up. Albert really didn't inspire confidence. "It's … it's in a safe place."

Albert felt like pouncing on Majid and shaking him until he gave him the information. But he didn't.

"Good, that's great," he said. "It's safer that way." He started rummaging, opening cupboard doors, poking about in the sideboard.

"What are you doing?"

"I need a drink. What have you got?"

"A drink?"

"Cognac, whisky…"

"My mum makes mint tea. But she's not here."

Albert sank into an armchair. "I guess it's just one of those days," he sighed. He closed his eyes for a moment, trying to think of a way to make the kid cooperate. He held out his cigarette packet. "Smoke? Nah, don't tell me – you've given up!"

Majid couldn't help laughing nervously. He didn't like Albert, but he admired his style.

"What's your girlfriend's name?"

Not sure whether to feel embarrassed or flattered, Majid said, "Are you talking about Aisha? She's just a friend from school."

"Well, she obviously likes you."

"Maybe," Majid conceded, modestly pulling a face.

"You didn't leave the computer at her place, by any chance?"

Majid shook his head.

"No? Good. Because you do realize ... *pffff*" – slowly Albert blew his cigarette smoke towards the ceiling – "the person who's got that machine ... *pffff*" – his blazing eyes met Majid's – "is in mortal danger."

Majid's gaze misted over. That scared feeling again. But he blinked and stiffened. No, he wouldn't say anything.

"I don't want any trouble for you, Majid, or your friends and family. And that's the truth."

Majid felt himself softening. Albert had saved him once, after all. He looked very big and strong. And very ready to hang about until Emmay got back. "Your computer's in Mr Mullins's flat."

"Who's that?"

"My English teacher." And then, trying to get his own back, Majid added, "He's the guy Nadia's after."

Albert gave a dirty smile. "Well, there's a funny coincidence. And where does he live, this prince charming?"

Twelve floors down, plus a few more steps, Samir was making his way through the basements of

Hummingbird Tower. He'd started off running. But now he was walking, because he was convinced he was already too late.

His responsibilities had never weighed as heavily on his shoulders as they did today. He'd take all the blame for what happened, of course. Lulu's safety was his job. Even when he wasn't there. He knew exactly what he was going to find. And what was going to happen next. There were no limits to the monster's appetite. Samir wouldn't be able to escape a third time. The monster had just been toying with him. Till now.

With each step, Samir prepared to join Lulu. He didn't see Prosper. Didn't even hear the boiler. There was just the long corridor left. The last one, that led to door 401.

As it turned out, he hadn't got there too late.

It was an extraordinary sight. Lulu was sitting calmly on a crate, bathed in a bluish light. Samir wanted to call to her but no sound came out of his mouth. The monster from the basements was towering over her, enormous and horrible. What was going on? How could Lulu watch the monster like that without flinching, without crying out in terror? Samir suddenly remembered the scary snake in *The Jungle Book*. Like Kaa, the monster appeared to hypnotize its prey.

Just then, Lulu held out her hand to the crackling creature and Samir woke from his stupor. "No!" he shouted. "Don't touch it! Whatever you do, don't touch it!"

Lulu looked round, apparently more frightened by Samir's outburst than by how close she was to the monster.

The monster who had also detected Samir's presence. Who pulled away from Lulu. Who fixed its dead eyes on the boy. Who shook its shapeless bulk.

Who came towards him.

"Don't hurt Samir!" Lulu shouted.

Poor Lulu. She obviously thought monsters obeyed orders.

"Don't hurt Samir!" she said again. "He doesn't mean any harm."

With his back glued to the damp basement wall, Samir realized he was going to die.

"Come here," said Lulu gently. "Come here. Leave Samir alone."

The monster seemed to waver, giving Samir two or three seconds to react. If only he'd had his flask of holy water on him. Between his numb fingers he could just feel the object he'd picked up by the dustbins. He was still holding Lulu's mug. In a flash of inspiration he ripped off the lid, the way you pull the pin out of a grenade, and threw the mug at the massive shape towering over him.

He had just enough time to notice that the monster had changed. It looked even stronger, more powerful. Its eyes and mouth were less like bottomless hollows now. It looked more human than when he and Sebastian had tried to exterminate it.

The water spurted out of the container.

"Don't!" howled Lulu.

Samir found himself on his backside, all the breath knocked out of him. He'd been deafened and blinded. It was Lulu's voice that brought him to his senses.

"Come back," she was whimpering. "Come back…"

Eventually he stood up and stumbled over to his little sister. He held her tight.

"You're evil! Evil!" she kept saying, hammering

her fists against his shoulder.

"It's over now," Samir whispered. "It won't hurt you any more."

"You killed him! You're the monster!"

"It's all over now," he repeated. "Come on, let's go." He wrapped his arms around Lulu's waist to lift her up.

"Leave me alone!" she yelled. "I can walk by myself! I can walk on my own!"

Lulu was shouting so loudly, Samir put her back down again. Instantly the little girl's legs gave way.

"You see," he said, catching her.

"You killed him. You killed him... The Force ... the Force..."

Lulu collapsed helplessly against Samir's chest. He picked her up again, but this time she didn't complain. She just lay limply in his arms.

It took a long time for Samir to make his way back through the basements. He kept staggering, his vision blurred by spasms of pure terror. Three times he stopped to make sure Lulu's heart was still beating. He climbed back up to their flat. He put his little sister down on her bed. He stood there for a long time, watching her. When a hint of pink came back into Lulu's cheeks, he finally relaxed.

"You know what," he said, "I don't think it needs to be holy – the water, I mean."

"It's burning me, it's burning me!" Lulu whimpered.

She had burn marks all over her body.

Best Buy!

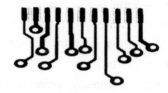

The small van hurtled along. Momo was sulking at the wheel. He'd asked for an assignment in East Timor. He'd landed one back in Moreland Town.

"Farting goo!" the cameraman exclaimed, punching the steering wheel.

"We'll call it noisy goo," said Emily Barter glumly.

"Noisy goo that makes kids hallucinate, right?"

"Apparently the dye comes off when you play with it, and the drug enters the body through the pores in the skin."

"So it's like that scare about cyanide in jars of baby food." His face lit up. He liked these kinds of stories. *The rumours are running riot. There's panic on the streets! Kids being drugged without realizing it. Parents who tell us: "We don't understand our son any more. He's changed..."* Momo was getting carried away. "Hey, didn't that police officer mention some special kind of farting goo?"

"Noisy goo," Emily corrected him, still looking fed up. "Yes, it was in the dead man's pocket in Hummingbird Tower."

Momo let out a whistle. "Either he was innocent, but knew too much about fart— noisy goo, or he was one of the baddies marketing a trial version."

Emily shrugged. She'd already had to cover a ridiculous story from Sunny-on-Sea about scorpions getting into egg boxes. There wasn't a single Sunnysider who'd ever seen a scorpion in an egg box, but everybody you asked knew the cousin of the grocer's husband who'd been stung by one.

"It's group hysteria," she insisted.

"Still, there's an unsolved murder," Momo reminded her. "And remember Hummingbird Tower? That girl who'd seen things along her corridor?"

"Yes. Plus there was that boy who mentioned

an electric ghost. The first thing we've got to do is find a tub of this tinted noisy goo," said Emily, cheering up. "So we can show one on air."

"We're in luck. Look over there!"

Momo drove into a car park. Next to B Power DIY and Big Action Sports, the words *Get the new farting goo here!* were emblazoned on a banner hung across the entrance to Big B Stores.

"See," said Momo. "All you've got to do is ask that bloke near the checkout."

That Bloke was none other than the manager of Moreland Town Big B Stores, Bernard Martin-Webber. He kept his customers under close surveillance from morning till night, because he was paranoid about shoplifters. And he hit the roof every time he saw all the Mustaphas and Mohammeds from the Moreland Estate going through the barriers without setting off the alarm.

"Er ... excuse me," said Momo, gently tapping the manager on the arm.

Martin-Webber leapt backwards. An armed attack: he'd been expecting this. Where was the security guard?

"Where's the noisy goo?" Momo asked.

"Isn't that big enough for you?" barked the manager, pointing to an enormous *Farting Goo* sign.

"Another basket case," sighed Momo.

Emily had already headed off. She stopped near a group of kids who were in front of the FG shelf.

"Ah, man!" cried one of them. "There's no orange."

"I've got a spare," said another. "D'you want to swap?"

"For what?"

"A coconut."

"Yeah, right," said the first kid in disgust.

They all snorted with laughter. A coconut was worth at least ten regular tubs.

Momo had hidden himself discreetly behind the sock shelf. *Best Buy: Three Pairs for the Price of One!* He was filming the discussion, the camera on his shoulder. Great – you could see how hooked the kids were.

"What about noisy goo that stains your hands?" Emily suddenly approached them. "Have you bought any of that?"

"Who's she?" asked one of them, stepping back.

"Don't go near her," said the smallest kid,

"she's evil. She's talking about the FG that makes you go crazy."

Emily didn't get a chance to explain herself before all the kids cleared off. So it looked like there *was* something in the rumour.

"We can't use much from that," grumbled Momo.

"Can you film the shelf, and zoom in on my hand grabbing a tub?" she asked him as she searched for a tub of the infamous tinted goo. Single colour, combo, fluorescent, scented and a novelty musical tub. But there was no sign of goo that stained. Unless it had slipped between all the other tubs.

Idly Momo lifted them up, shook them, put them back down again. "What do people see in rubbish like this? I don't get it. These kids must be brainwashed."

Albert knew what people saw in rubbish like that. He'd been very well paid to know.

The automatic doors of Big B Stores slid open. The manager immediately gave the strong type in the crumpled suit a suspicious look. Albert stared back. He could spot a B Corp worker a mile off.

He usually avoided public places, but since he'd met Nadia, the fact he'd been wearing the same socks for over a week was getting him down. His eye was caught by the best buy sign. His finances were running low.

As he was heading towards the checkout with three pairs of socks in his hands, Albert noticed the cameraman filming the kids. His heart did a somersault as he spotted the huge shelf of farting goo. He heard Emily and the kids talking about the kind of FG that drove you crazy. What was the story? Had B Corp really pushed their experiment that far? How could he find out without taking too many risks?

I need a pawn, Albert thought as he left Big B Stores. Somebody who can act in my place. He smiled. He'd just remembered his schooldays and, by association, Nadia Martin. Then he frowned, as he thought about Mr Mullins, who'd already got his computer and who, according to Majid, wasn't far off getting the science teacher too.

Albert, in love? He scowled. No, he just wanted Nadia to know he wasn't a complete nobody. He wasn't a teacher in some godforsaken dump of a school. Of course, there were one or two things weighing on his conscience. But they were behind him now and, in any case, it was always the uptight girls who went for the bad guys. Which meant Albert would win hands down.

He changed his socks under the awning of a pizzeria, much to the amazement of the people eating. Then he headed off at a brisk pace to the old part of Moreland Town, where Mr Mullins lived. Time to check out the lie of the land.

"And then," he said between gritted teeth, "may the best man win!"

The Monster's Bride

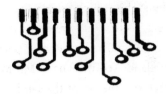

Samir was worried about Lulu. Not her physical well-being. Her burn marks had healed quickly and some of her strength was back. She'd even decided to practise walking by leaning against the walls. But she was going mad. Lulu wanted to walk so she could visit the monster in the basements again.

"It's dead," Samir told her, not sounding convinced.

She shook her head mysteriously and whispered, "He's just hungry."

According to Lulu, the monster ate electricity. It was responsible for all the power failures in the building. As soon as it had eaten enough, it would become as big and strong as before.

"Maybe even stronger!" she said excitedly. "And he'll share the Force with me."

Samir had been able to carry his little sister up the stairs, but his secret was too much of a weight on his mind. So he told Sebastian.

"And Lulu wants to go back to find the monster again?"

"That's all she thinks about. She says it's very gentle with her."

"Is she in love?"

Weird question. Samir made a disgusted face. "She says it talks to her inside her head," he admitted. "She's trying to find a name for it, because she thinks it's sad it hasn't got one."

"She's in love," Sebastian confirmed. He seemed to be very focused on this point. A monster. A girl. They fall in love. He pressed a thumb and index finger against his eyelids, and concentrated harder. "Got it," he murmured, opening his eyes. "*The Bride of Frankenstein.*"

"What?"

"In *The Bride of Frankenstein*, the monster falls in love with a girl. I've seen the film, but the details are a bit fuzzy." He shut his eyes again.

"If it's anything like transcommunication…" grumbled Samir.

Sebastian pretended not to hear. He adopted the sing-song voice of a clairvoyant. *"The monster goes into the forest… There's a blind hermit. The hermit plays the violin to calm the monster… That's it! We've got to play the violin to the monster in the basements."*

"Will it work better than holy water?" Samir wondered .

"The monster can't be destroyed," said Sebastian in the same faraway voice. *"But it can be tamed and taught to talk.* That's how it works in the film. The first word it says is *friend."* He turned to Samir and added, "It's just as well I've been learning the violin for two years."

Samir was in a hurry to get home. He was afraid of leaving Lulu alone for too long. She'd promised not to go down to the basements again without telling him, but these days she seemed more likely to obey the monster than her brother.

"Lulu! Lulu? Ah, you're there…"

The little girl was in the kitchen, spreading

some jam on a piece of toast. Samir watched her in silence.

"You're standing up," he pointed out at last.

"Yes."

"You're doing it all by yourself? You're not leaning against anything?"

"You can see for yourself."

Lulu even did a little dance. She'd got used to the idea by now. Samir found it unbelievable. His little sister had been in bed and in pain for as long as he could remember.

"D'you think it's still in the basements?" he whispered.

"Yes." She lifted a hand to one ear. "He's calling me."

"It knows your name?"

Lulu thought about this for a moment. "He doesn't know that people have names," she said gently. She took a bite of toast and added, "He doesn't know what words are."

"It hasn't got a brain," scoffed Samir. He was jealous of the monster.

His sister gave him a stern look. "You mustn't say that. He's like ... a baby. Babies don't know

what words are. But I'm going to teach him to talk."
She laid a tiny hand on her brother's. "I have to go
back there. D'you understand? He hasn't got any
friends. He doesn't even know what friends are."

"*The Bride of Frankenstein*," whispered Samir, feeling
overwhelmed. Everything was turning out just as
Sebastian had predicted. "Listen, Lulu, if you really
want to go back there—"

"Yes." Her eyes sparkled.

"Don't go on your own. I'll come with you."

"But you'll kill him again," she protested.

"No, I won't. We'll play it the violin."

They arranged to meet Sebastian on Saturday
afternoon. There was no danger of anybody inter-
rupting their trip to the basements. The tenants
didn't dare go down there any more, not since the
dead body had been discovered. The caretaker had
thought about padlocking the door again, but he
was so fed up with all the vandalism that he'd
dropped the idea. So they just pushed open the
heavy wooden door and walked down the steps.

Lulu went first. She was so delicate and frail she
hardly seemed to touch the ground. Samir lit her

way and Sebastian brought up the rear, his violin case tucked under his arm. Lulu's confidence in the monster had almost set her big brother's mind at rest. But he turned to Sebastian all the same and whispered, "Are you sure about the vio—"

"In the film…"

Samir shrugged. He'd brought some water with him, without telling anybody.

As they got closer to lot 401, they heard a strange moaning sound, a pained, gagged mmhh-mmm sound. A sharp click made Samir jump. Sebastian was opening his violin case.

"There you are!" said Lulu cheerfully. "Wow, you've grown!"

The monster had refuelled. It was a clumsy lump in the middle of lot 401, swaying to the rhythm of the moaning noise it was making. Lulu went over and put her hand on its arm. Straight away they both started crackling and Lulu's curly hair stood on end like a crazy crow's nest.

"You're not so floppy now," she noticed, feeling her friend's biceps.

The monster was more solid, and its shape more defined. It didn't look like a cloud or candyfloss any longer. More like a giant rubber buoy pumped up with electricity.

Samir and Sebastian hung back by the entrance.

"D'you think it can see us?" Samir whispered.

The words were barely out of his mouth before the monster turned towards him with a blank expression. It was becoming increasingly like the golem from the game, the creature Hugh called Joke. And its stitched eyes and gashed mouth made it look like a distant relation of Frankenstein's monster.

"Mmmmh!" it wailed. Was it sad? Was it trying to say something? It gestured towards the two boys, as if pointing them out to Lulu. Did it recognize Samir as the person who'd thrown water at it?

"Play the violin," he squeaked.

Sebastian wedged the instrument under his chin, closed his eyes for a moment, brandished his bow and proceeded to make a dreadful miaowing sound followed by a hideous screeching. It was the "Allegro" from Suzuki Violin Book Two.

"Huhuhuh…" wailed the monster. "Huhuhuh." It backed towards the wall.

"Stop it!" Lulu shouted, looking aghast at

Sebastian. "Can't you see you're scaring him?"

"But in the film…" complained Sebastian, lowering his bow.

The poor monster had collapsed in a huddle. It looked in a bad way.

"He's losing his strength," sighed Lulu. She was wobbling as well, and had to lean against the wall. "I'm going to fall," she said, looking as miserable as the hunched monster.

Samir now did something very brave. He went over to the creature, holding out his torch at arm's length. The torch seemed to vanish as soon as it came into contact with the monster, and Samir received a shock that sent him reeling. In a flash the monster was back on its feet again.

"Say thank you," Lulu reminded it, standing strong again too.

"Mmmmh," chanted the monster as it waddled about.

Sebastian had watched the whole episode, his pupils dilated with a mixture of fear and curiosity. Nothing he'd ever read about the paranormal was any use in identifying this kind of phenomenon. "It's an electric ectoplasm," he said, trying to sound scientific. "It uses electricity to regenerate itself, and disconnects when it comes into contact with water."

It sounded good, but it didn't explain much.

In the meantime, the grown-ups were coming up with a few explanations of their own.

Who Knows?

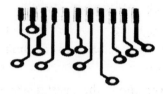

Mrs Mullins was a psychologist. Psychology had taught her that watching TV at mealtimes is bad for family relationships. But Hugh had been a grown-up for some years now. So when he turned on the TV before sitting down to supper, his mother just sighed.

"Just a rumour, or is there cause for concern? Can there really be smoke without fire?" asked the newsreader. "Emily Barter reports." Grey concrete towers broken up by nondescript patches of land appeared on the screen. "An estate just like any other," came the voice-over, "with its lifts that don't work…"

"It's the Moreland Estate," shouted Hugh, jumping up from his chair.

"They're not still going on about the body in Hummingbird Tower?" tutted Mrs Mullins. "Why do they always blow these stories out of all propor—"

"Shh! Look, it's Big B Stores."

Sure enough, there was the main entrance to the supermarket with its banner proclaiming: *Get the new farting goo here!*

"After Pokémon, the latest craze in the playground is noisy goo," the reporter continued as the camera zoomed in on the shelves of multicoloured tubs.

"Yes, my son he iz collecting," a housewife told the camera. "Iz childrin for you. Fashion it iz so big deal."

"It's Mrs Badach!" exclaimed Hugh.

Emily Barter had interviewed Majid's mum for half an hour, and edited out everything except those three bland sentences.

"But over the last few weeks," the journalist went on, "a strange rumour has been circulating among the young people and alarming their parents. Could there be a toxic substance inside certain tubs of tinted noisy goo? And could it trigger hallucinations when it comes into contact with the children's skin?"

During her voice-over, a man with a worried expression appeared on the screen. Dr Donald. Paediatrician. "One very anxious mother made an appointment with me," revealed Dr Donald. "Her daughter claimed to have seen electric smoke—" He was about to launch into a long explanation when the picture cut abruptly to an outside shot. Kids playing football.

"What about you?" Emily asked one of them. "Have you seen strange things around here too?"

"It's Mamadou's brother!" shouted Hugh.

The kid was posing with his hands on his hips. "It ain't me, it's like me bro's bluds."

Subtitles appeared. *It was not me. It was my brother's friends.*

"What did they see?"

"A tric-elec ster-mon!" said the boy, cracking up.

"And had they bought any noisy goo?"

"Nuff tubs, innit!"

Dazzling proof. The report finished with a trip back to Big B Stores, where the exasperated manager,

Bernard Martin-Webber, was shouting at the invisible cameraman. "Move on, please! There's nothing to see here!"

Stunned, Hugh and his mother looked at each other.

"Did you understand any of that?" Mrs Mullins asked.

"Well, 8D are certainly saying some crazy things these days."

Mrs Mullins's face tensed. She thought back to the transcommunication session. Her son's behaviour had been worrying her for a while now. He had a wild look about him every time he emerged from his study. Worse still, he never went out any more, never saw anybody. And then there were those little holes in the study carpet, like cigarette burns. And that strange smell that had spread through the flat. Marijuana or not marijuana? Mrs Mullins was worried.

When she went out to do her shopping, she was reluctant to leave Hugh on his own. "Haven't you got any friends to go and see?" she hinted.

"Friends?" Hugh headed off into his study

without further comment. He had enemies, that was what he had. The evening before, the Evildoers had taken two lives off Natasha, who didn't have her dragon to protect her any more. Much to Calimero's annoyance, Bubble hadn't come back.

"Well, *hello* there!"

There was Natasha on his screen, waiting for him. She waved. Hugh gave a tired smile. She wore him out, that girl. Just as he was about to sit down, the doorbell startled him out of his lethargy. He thought it would be Majid. Magic Berber was his only friend.

It wasn't.

"Hello. I'd like to speak to Mr Mullins," said the man on the landing.

Gordon Freeman, thought Hugh. One of his heroes was standing slap bang in front of him. Over six feet tall, with wrestler's shoulders, and so good-looking he could only mean trouble.

"Are you Mr Mullins?"

"Yes… Yes, I am. What's this about?"

"It's personal. Can I come in?" Without waiting for an answer, the man pushed Hugh back into the flat with his fingertips. He'd sized him up straight away. Small build, practically a teenager still. And Nadia was in love with that?

"Are you Albert?" Hugh asked suddenly.

Amused, the strong type winked. "So Majid's told you about me? Where's my computer?"

Hugh could smell trouble. This guy had come to take it off him. His veins flooded with unfamiliar courage as he clenched his fists. "Now look here, unless you can prove otherwise, we're talking about my computer."

"Or Majid's, at any rate."

"We did a swap. Anyway, it's none of your business."

Albert towered over him, but if Hugh was trembling it was from anger not fear. Albert misjudged the situation. He thought he had Hugh at his mercy. He shoved him again, jabbing a finger into his shoulder.

"Listen, this game's too dangerous for you. There are hired killers out there looking for this machine, so why don't you just give it back to me without a fuss, and I'll make sure you're saved a lot of aggro."

Thanks to Samir, Hugh was used to standing

his ground despite feeling inferior. "What hired killers?" he asked. "And whose side are you on anyway?"

"The less you know, my friend, the better."

"Don't patronize me!" Hugh protested indignantly. Then, as if it was Mamadou standing in front of him, he added, "Leave the room immediately!"

Albert was taken aback. He examined Hugh's face. Blue eyes, unruly hair, the expression of a stubborn kid. He could feel his jealousy rekindling. This was a more serious rival than he'd realized. Of course, he could easily smash Hugh's cute face with his knuckleduster or use his flick knife to widen his smile. But Nadia wouldn't approve.

"OK," he agreed, "let's cool it. I'll explain what's going on." He sat down in an armchair and with a click of his fingers signalled for Hugh to sit opposite. "I'm the computer programmer who created Golem," he began.

Hugh laid down his weapons. "Wow!" he said admiringly. "But I'm having a small problem with it just now. Why do you make Bubble disappear? The little dragon, I mean."

"I don't make him disappear."

"Oh yes you do! Come and see for yourself."

Albert jumped at the chance of laying his hands on his computer again.

"Well, hello there!"

Hugh had clicked on Natasha. He was immediately back in the game, picking up where he'd left off.

"Unbelievable!" whispered Albert, his eyes glued to the screen.

"That's what I'm telling you," crowed Hugh. "The dragon's gone."

Albert looked at him furiously. "What on earth's this game doing here anyway?" he shouted. "Nobody else was supposed to be able to access it. How did you manage?"

"I didn't do anything," Hugh shouted back. "Your game kept popping up to bug me. It made it impossible to work!"

The two men were on the verge of coming to blows.

"And that girl drives me crazy!"

"Which girl?" asked Albert, thinking of Nadia.

"Her, of course." Hugh pointed at Natasha.

Albert let out a wolf whistle and clicked on Natasha.

"Well, *hello* there!"

Albert laughed. The girl-golem was an inspired blend. A cross between Catwoman and Lara Croft. He sized Hugh up and gave him a mental age of thirteen. He turned back to the game and noticed that, sure enough, the little dragon had disappeared. "Unbelievable," he said again. "There's something going on…"

That "something" had begun a few months earlier, when Albert was working at B Corp HQ. On several occasions he had noticed his game suddenly launching itself for no reason, as if somebody had been tampering with it. Was there a traitor in his team? Or just a brilliant hoaxer?

"This game wasn't meant to be for sale yet," he said finally. "It was being kept top secret. We weren't even allowed to discuss it with specialist magazines."

"Well, all the kids are playing it at school, I can tell you that for a fact."

"And all the kids are buying farting goo, aren't they?"

Hugh nodded, although he didn't see what that had to do with it.

"It was supposed to be an experiment," Albert said slowly, as if trying to justify it to himself, "an enquiry into human behaviour. I agreed to it … just to see what'd happen." He'd also agreed to it because the work was incredibly well paid, but he didn't mention that.

"What did you agree to?"

"Inserting a subliminal image into my game."

"Image?"

"You know what I mean: slipping an image that doesn't have anything to do with the subject matter into a filmed sequence. The photo of a presidential candidate appearing in the middle of a Bond film, for instance. But the image flashes up so quickly you don't really see it. You just register it subconsciously."

"And the point of all this is?"

Albert looked embarrassed and coughed. "To … manipulate people. They register the message 'vote so-and-so' without realizing it, and they … well, they vote so-and-so. The thing is, I didn't really believe in it. I thought it was as phoney as truth serum. There's no scientific evidence, no proof."

"And what was the subliminal message in your game?" asked Hugh, who'd already got a pretty good idea.

Albert laughed nervously. "Something about farting goo."

"*Buy Big Brand farting goo,*" Hugh said. "So now do you believe in subliminal advertising?"

Albert didn't answer. The kids were buying farting goo, which was certainly one of the most moronic products ever marketed. But there'd been lots of other fads, from stickers to playing cards. It was all about following a trend.

Suddenly he noticed a range of multicoloured tubs stacked above the computer. "Are you collecting them?"

"Clearly," snapped Hugh. "So's my mum. No scientific evidence, no proof, hey?"

Part of Albert wanted to laugh. But he knew subliminal images containing a message from an obscure sect had been detected in a Japanese animation series. He also knew that subliminal phrases like "Relax!" and "Go on, treat yourself!" were played through the in-store muzak of certain supermarkets. It was purely experimental, of course. But it only had one goal: mental manipulation.

"In any case, I refused to go through with it," said Albert, who didn't like being cast as the villain. "I could see that anybody playing my game became obsessed by it, which risked increasing the impact of the subliminal image. If you register the same message unconsciously ten, twenty, fifty times, it ends up leaving its mark."

Hugh was staring darkly at his tubs of farting goo. He'd bin them all. Then he glanced at Albert. He still wanted an answer to one important question: whose side was he on? He decided to put Albert to the test.

"The police will need telling about this, won't they?"

"And have them seal off our computer?"

The two men smiled at each other. They were half allies, half enemies. Neither wanted to lose the computer, even if Golem was now available in the school library and elsewhere. The press were talking about it as if it was a new Internet virus. But it had all started with this electric blue computer.

"By the way, while you're here," said Hugh,

"you can help me reach the next level. I've lost two lives and the stakes are just too high."

"Hold on a minute. There's a slight problem," Albert warned.

Another problem?

"I didn't have time to finish it."

"No!" shouted Hugh. "No, no way, you can't say that!" He didn't feel let down or frustrated. He felt horror. Despair. For hours at a time, days on end, Calimero had battled obsessively to win a soul for Natasha.

"So you mean," he said, stretching his arms out towards the screen, "she'll never be able ... she'll never have..." He knew he was making a fool of himself. But he carried on. "She'll never be free."

Albert gazed at the multicoloured tubs neatly arranged on the shelf. "And you think *we* are?"

Pa-aa-arty Time

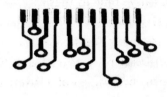

"When are we going back?" Lulu wanted to know.

"Wednesday," Samir decided. "But nobody must find out. It's our secret. Let's not talk about it any more."

"The monster in the basements is a hallucination triggered by farting goo." Sebastian sniggered. "That's what they said on TV." He and Samir, who had become inseparable, were in Lulu's bedroom.

"You'll have to pretend you're still sick," Samir warned his kid sister.

Lulu smiled distractedly. The Force hadn't totally deserted her, but her legs had been feeling like cotton wool since this morning. It was Sunday, and she could sense the monster getting weaker down in lot 401. "It'd be a good idea to take him something to eat," she said.

Supplying food for the electric ectoplasm, as Sebastian called it, was proving difficult. The lift and timer-switches for the lights were permanently on the blink, and the caretaker couldn't be bothered mending them or changing the fuses.

By Monday evening Lulu could only move around by clinging to the furniture. She didn't complain, but pain was gradually taking over from the Force.

"When the monster's feeling good, Lulu's good," Samir told Sebastian. "When the monster's feeling bad, Lulu's bad."

Sebastian was sifting through his mental notes again, muttering, "Bad ... bad, good ... good. *The Yellow Mark!*" he exclaimed suddenly.

"What are you on about?"

"In *The Yellow Mark* by E. P. Jacobs, Professor Septimus manages to control his human guinea pig by connecting to the megawave of its brain." It was clear as day to him. "The monster is connected to the megawave of your sister's brain."

Samir didn't say anything, but he was beginning

to wonder if there wasn't an alien hijacking Sebastian's brain.

On Tuesday morning Samir skipped school and went to Big B Stores. He'd decided to steal as many light bulbs as he could so the monster could have a proper snack. When he found the right aisle, he chose round bulbs, a hundred and fifty watts, plus some halogen striplights, to vary the menu. His jacket doubled in volume. Since he couldn't go through the checkout empty-handed, he grabbed a packet of Special B cereal bearing the slogan *Refuel your energy*. Maybe the monster could eat it for dessert.

Samir was too busy with his loot to notice one of the store detectives mingling discreetly with the customers. But the detective had spotted him. He'd nab the kid at the checkout. Being familiar with his boss's tastes, he decided to win Mr Martin-Webber's approval by forewarning him.

"Are we talking dreadlocks?"

"No, couscous."

As he was heading towards the checkout, Samir saw Mrs Badach. Majid's mum recognized him and gave him a faint smile. She wasn't a fan of her son's classmate. She was just starting to unload her trolley at the checkout, when she saw the detective go up to Samir. At the same time, the manager was closing in on the guilty party, signalling for Samir to open his jacket.

"Excuze me," Mrs Badach said to the cashier, "my son he iz looking for me. Samir! Samir!" She was practically running as she called out his name. Crimson-faced, Samir was tugging at his jacket zip.

"Samir, here iz me!" cried Mrs Badach, her heart pounding. "Hello, mister. Iz my son, Samir. You iz not taking trolley?" She caught a glimpse of the light bulbs Samir was clasping in his arms. "Good. You find" – she faltered, shocked to see just how much he had stolen – "light bulbs for your father. Well done, my son. Excuze me, mister, my son he haz not trolley habit. Iz childrin for you…"

Still talking and still being watched by the flabbergasted store detective and manager, she dragged Samir over to the checkout.

"Excuze me," she said to the cashier. "To put it, my son. And for cereal too. There we go. How much it iz?"

At the exit, Samir tried to find the words to thank Mrs Badach but couldn't, so he took the bag full of light bulbs that she held out to him in silence.

"Iz not good to steal, Samir," she told him.

He could see she felt sorry for him. Maybe she thought he'd been pressured into doing it. Dealing stuff for a crew on the estate. Samir wanted to tell her everything. About the monster, and Lulu, and the mobile phone he'd stolen from the dead body. About how frightened he'd been, and how lonely he felt. But Mrs Badach had gone. Humiliated, Samir consoled himself with the thought that he'd only stolen to save Lulu.

Hugh was also wrestling with good and bad that day. His recent "partnership" with Albert had left him strapped for cash. The guy was a scrounger, a rogue who'd sold his talents to B Corp.

But what exactly was B Corp? A multinational organization that used subliminal messaging to brainwash its young and impressionable customers? It was a market leader in high-tech electronics and telecommunications, as well as owning supermarket chains, sports shops, a range of food products and a line of computers and games. But was it really just another conglomerate? B Corp had successfully infiltrated Moreland Town, and you could also find it in the hip districts of London, Paris and New York, along with its slogan *Life is Big B*. Nothing out of the ordinary there. Except that B Corp also used hired killers to retrieve its computers and track down its former employees, which *was* kind of out of the ordinary.

After meeting Albert, Hugh had signed up to evening classes and joined a gym. But he was a dreamer by nature, and hoped there was a faster way of transforming himself into a hero. Why not explore the basements of Hummingbird Tower in search of the monster? It couldn't be too dangerous, considering that the chances of the monster really existing were approximately zero.

So, on Wednesday afternoon, Hugh set off for Hummingbird Tower. He tried to copy Albert's swagger. First fright: running into the caretaker and his dog in the main entrance hall.

"Are you looking for somebody?"

"No. Yes," stammered Hugh. "Er ... Mrs Badach."

"Twelfth floor. But I'm warning you, the lift's out of order."

Hugh climbed two floors before tiptoeing back down again. The caretaker had gone out, and the way to the basements was clear. Let the adventure begin. He congratulated himself on having had the foresight to bring a torch. The timer-switch for the lights wasn't working any more than the lift.

Second fright: Prosper. The cleverly drawn ghost made him jump when he turned the corner. Then there was the gurgling boiler, the scurrying of a rat, and a creaking sound of dubious origin. With each noise, Hugh's heart pounded in his chest.

The young English teacher passed the open door of lot 401 and flashed his torch inside. The monster was at the back, sluggish and lifeless. Hugh didn't see it and headed on deeper into the basements.

All of a sudden he thought he heard whispering. Was somebody there? He certainly didn't want any Hummingbird Tower residents catching him. What a scandal if his colleagues discovered he was hanging out in tower block basements. Or what if it was a crew? There were so many rumours about the

Moreland Estate. Hugh was completely freaked out, and hid in lot 412.

The crew in question consisted of Samir and Sebastian, who were carrying Lulu between them. The little girl couldn't walk any more. She was clenching her teeth so no cries of pain would escape her lips. Samir had the light bulbs and cereal in his backpack.

"Where is it?" asked Sebastian, peering into lot 401.

"Against the wall," said Lulu sadly. "Poor thing! He's all floppy again." Her friend's sorry state made her forget her own suffering.

"We'll pump him back up in no time," Samir reassured her as he opened his rucksack. "There we go, a hundred and fifty watts, yum, yum..." He'd suffered enough electric shocks by now, so he decided to toss the bulbs at the monster like a ring-master chucking fish to a performing seal. "Catch, big boy!"

Ting, ting... The bulb smashed on the concrete floor. "We need to put in some practice," Samir admitted, moving closer.

The second attempt wasn't much better. The

bulb vanished when it came into contact with the monster, but with no result.

"Aargh, man!" Samir lost his temper. "And they're worth nuff dollars, these bulbs!" He dug out another one and prepared to try one last time.

Sebastian grabbed his arm. "There's no point."

"D'you think it'd prefer the halogen ones?"

"No, it wants electric current. It wants energy."

Samir got the packet of Special B cereal out of his bag, and Sebastian sighed pityingly.

"What, then?" Samir fumed.

"My torch'd do the trick, because it's switched on," Sebastian explained.

"Yeah, right. Then we'll be left in the dark with…" Samir jerked his head towards the monster.

"Would batteries work?" asked Lulu. "I've got some in my Furby."

"Your what?" said Sebastian.

"It's a furry toy that talks," explained Samir. "You put batteries in it."

According to Sebastian, that was exactly what the monster needed: batteries to recharge it.

Samir rushed back up to the flat to look for his sister's furry toy. As soon as he'd grabbed it, the

Furby opened its eyes and said, "Me still sleepy."

"Sorry," Samir told it. "There's a monster waiting for you." Without bothering to take the batteries out, he tore down the stairs.

"Yippee-yay!" The Furby burst out laughing, because it was all shaken up. "It's pa-aa-arty time!"

"Shut it!" Samir said good-naturedly.

Back in lot 401, he held the furry creature out to Sebastian.

"Yippee-yay!" said the Furby. "It's pa-aa-arty time!"

"What's it on about?" asked Sebastian.

"Don't take any notice. Just get the batteries out."

Sebastian examined the little door that covered the batteries. "You got a screwdriver?"

Samir put his head in his hands.

"Yippee-yay!" squealed the Furby. "It's pa—"

The poor toy didn't get a chance to finish. Samir lost his temper and knocked it out of Sebastian's hands. The Furby twirled gracefully in mid-air before exploding on contact with the monster.

"It's swelling up, it's swelling up!" shouted

Samir as the electric ectoplasm recharged itself.

"My Furby!" whispered Lulu sadly. But she wasn't sad for long. The Force was back and her friend the monster was on his feet again.

"Hug me!"

The children shuddered. Who'd said that?

"Me still sleepy."

"It's that stupid Furby," muttered Samir, searching for it on the ground.

"Cock-a-doodle-doo! The sun's come out to play!"

All three children stared at the monster.

"It's him!" exclaimed Lulu. "He's talking in Furby-speak."

"This is going to be a laugh," Samir grumbled.

Suddenly Sebastian switched off his torch. "Shh!"

They weren't alone. Something had just fallen over in the corridor.

"Turn it back on," begged Samir.

"Shh," Sebastian hissed again.

They could hear breathing. And they could make out a faint glimmer, the kind you get from a torch somebody's trying to hide.

"Yippee-yay! It's pa-aa-arty time!" threw in the delighted monster.

"Who ... who's there?" came an unconfident male voice.

"Cock-a-doodle-doo!" replied the monster. Arguably not the most relevant response.

"I don't want to hurt you," said the man, sounding more concerned about not getting hurt himself.

Sebastian switched on the torch again and looked at Samir. The voice was familiar. "Is that you, sir?" He went towards the door of lot 401 and saw his English teacher standing in the corridor, wide-eyed with terror.

"Sebastian!" said Hugh, sounding relieved. "So you're the ones who've been playing in the basements." He glanced at the floor. "What got broken? Bottles?"

"No, light bulbs. Wait! Stay there. You'll get a shock," Sebastian warned him.

"A big shock," Samir added.

Hugh shook his head. His students had clearly gone mad.

Little Lulu slipped between the two boys. "Don't

hurt him," she begged. "He's a monster, but he's really sweet."

The three kids were blocking the entrance to lot 401. What were they trying to hide?

"What's going on?" Hugh pushed Samir aside. He took a step, he saw, he shouted. "The … there's … a…" His legs gave way, and he groped for the wall. "Joke," he said in the voice of a dying man, "it's Joke."

Calimero had recognized his screen mate. Except this golem's head touched the ceiling.

Lulu smiled at the monster. "There you go, you've got a name. It's Joke."

"Yippee-yay! It's pa-aa-arty time!" answered Joke.

For a moment, Hugh thought he was going to pass out. But his students seemed so calm, he managed to pull himself together.

"It's an electric ectoplasm, sir," Sebastian explained.

"No, it's not," stammered Hugh, "it's a hallucination." The previous evening, he'd pummelled some farting goo before throwing it in the bin. He was hallucinating.

"Don't touch it, sir!" Samir shouted.

Hugh had stuck out his hand to reassure himself there really was nothing there. He got a shock that sent him flying back.

"That was a big one!" Samir grinned, an old hand when it came to shocks. "Are you OK, sir?"

"Let's get out of here. We've got to run for our lives!" Hugh tugged at Sebastian's arm. "Get a move on, quickly!"

Their teacher's panic was catching. They ran. They kept bumping into one another as they raced through the basements towards the exit. When they reached the door Hugh turned the knob. Once. Twice.

"We're locked in," he whispered, too terrified to react.

"We can't be, sir!" said Samir. He had a go. "It must be the caretaker. He's put the padlock back."

"Yippee-yay! It's pa-aa-arty time!"

Hugh turned round, his back jammed against the door. The monster had followed them, and Lulu was holding it by the hand.

"Let go! Let go!" Hugh gabbled at the little girl. "It'll electrocute you."

"Oh no it won't," said Samir confidently. "The monster's connected to my sister's megawave."

"Don't say 'the monster' any more," Lulu told him. "He's called Joke. Aren't you, Joke?"

"Hug me!" said Joke.

"I'm going crazy," murmured Hugh.

"One thing's for sure," said Sebastian. "We're locked in."

"Why don't we just knock on the door?" Lulu suggested.

Hugh immediately pictured the scene: the crowd of tenants, the caretaker arriving with his dog, Joke making his grand entrance, general pandemonium. "I've left my mobile at home," he moaned, "or I could have rung my mother."

Samir shivered. "I've got one."

The others stared at him in amazement, but none of them saw him blush in the dark as he got the phone he'd taken from the corpse out of his pocket. It was still charged up, but Samir hadn't dared use it till now. After all, it was a dead person's mobile.

"Call Majid," Sebastian suggested.

"Er ... yeah."

Samir didn't even know how the mobile worked. He pressed a button with a little green phone on it. Twice, to make sure. A number appeared on the screen. He didn't realize it, but it was the last number dialled by Sven, the murdered B Corp worker.

"Hey, it's ringing!" he said in surprise, putting the phone to his ear.

"Yeah?" muttered an arrogant voice at the other end.

Samir didn't know whether to say hello or ask for help.

"Who is it?" he asked.

The Party Goes On!

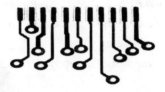

Mrs Badach looked approvingly at the manager of Big B Stores, her hands resting on her shopping trolley. "You iz looking nice today. Iz for party?"

"You what? Oh yes, right, a party."

For at least the tenth time that day Bernard Martin-Webber, BMW to his friends, checked to see if his royal blue tie was hanging straight over his finely striped shirt. With his linen suit just back from the dry-cleaner's and his pointy Italian shoes, he felt ready to face the day ahead.

"So iz true? You give me hundred quid?"

"Fifty," the manager quickly corrected.

"Yes, fifty. You give it me?"

"In Big B Stores vouchers, for next time."

Mrs Badach could hardly believe her luck. Before today, the best thing she'd ever got from Big B Stores had been a discount voucher for twenty pence off a tub of Big Clean washing powder.

"And I walk round supermarkit with your big deal gear on my head, innit?"

BMW's eyes nearly popped out of his head. But he repeated the instructions with uncharacteristic patience. She should just do her shopping as normal and select the items she wanted.

"There you go," he said, putting a kind of hard hat on her head. "Now if you'll excuse me, Fatima, I've got a big afternoon ahead."

"Kamera iz on top? But I iz not going to watch your tellie programme."

"Don't worry, it won't leave the premises. It's an experiment. To make the store even better."

Mrs Badach pushed her trolley off down an aisle. She couldn't understand why anybody would be interested in watching a film featuring tins of peas and rolls of loo paper. During her shopping spree, she was surprised to bump into four other people also wearing hard hats with miniature cameras mounted on top.

Bull's-eye! BMW congratulated himself on putting together the perfect sample group: Fatima, a young executive, a granny and two housewives in the under-fifties category. He checked his tie again. Then he glanced at his watch. The B Corp bigwigs would be here in less than an hour. Enough time for him to regret being so generous.

"I must be mad," he cursed. "Fifty quid. Those morons would have done it for a packet of Yummy B sweets!"

But BMW wasn't feeling quite himself today. And when he saw the black limousine pull into the store's private car park, he could feel damp patches spreading from the armpits of his carefully pressed striped shirt. The manager of Big B Stores at Sunny-on-Sea had committed suicide shortly after the B Corp bigwigs paid him a visit. No connection, of course.

As planned, there were three B Corp workers, including the bodyguard. But they weren't the conventional young business types BMW had been expecting. Instead he found himself shaking hands with Mr Rawalpindi and a woman with short grey hair who simply introduced herself as Alicia.

BMW took them into the conference room. The bodyguard stood next to the door.

"As you know," Mr Rawalpindi began, "your Big B Store is in one of our eight test zones. Like the one in Sunny-on-Sea."

A click of metal made BMW jump. The bodyguard had just opened the blade of his flick knife to clean his nails. He was a young guy with white hair. An albino.

"We've analysed your results," Mr Rawalpindi went on. "There's nothing outstanding about your sales figures."

"Shoplifting is down," Martin-Webber protested weakly.

"Shoplifting's only natural in a store like this," Alicia commented. "If the number of thefts drops, it means people don't want our products badly enough."

Martin-Webber studied the woman's face carefully. She wasn't joking. "I'm sorry, Alicia, but I think you'll find it's chiefly due to the quality of our video surveillance system. Let me just show you…"

BMW pressed one of the buttons on his remote control and an ugly grey image appeared on a monitor. A hand could be seen grabbing a CD from a display unit. The next shot showed the contents of a shopping trolley.

"There!" he crowed. "He didn't put that CD in his trolley. We caught our couscous-eating friend at the checkout." The colour drained from his racist face as he met Mr Rawalpindi's impassive gaze.

"Did he pay?" Alicia asked calmly.

"Of course. It was either that or get the police involved. We know how to talk to cousc— shoplifters."

"So he's a good customer, then," Alicia continued. "A customer who pays is a good customer."

Click, click. Chalk Face was playing with his flick knife. A look of irritation flashed across Alicia's face. BMW turned his attention back to the screen. The next sequence involved the hardware section. They saw a man deliberating for a long time in front of a shelf of padlocks.

"That's the caretaker of Hummingbird Tower.

He's honest. Dim as you like, but honest."

"Our customers are never dim," Alicia told him. Her voice was like a diamond slicing through glass.

The manager clearly wasn't on the same wavelength as the B Corp bigwigs. He was cooking in his own sweat like a piece of meat in its juice.

"Shall we take a look at what the video hats are filming?" suggested Mr Rawalpindi.

"Hold on!" came a voice from near the door.

They looked round. Chalk Face was pointing his knife at the screen. "There, I think I saw... The guy in the last sequence. Would you mind rewinding it?"

"Would you mind leaving?" said Alicia icily.

"Look, the guy I just saw on the video—"

"Out!" she roared.

The bodyguard left the room. BMW pressed play for the next recording. "It's almost live," he explained.

Unappealing images of tins and bottles filmed by the five members of the sample group appeared on the screen. The B Corp bigwigs examined the different sequences with rapt concentration, as if they were expecting to see aliens rise up out of the frozen-foods counter.

"Excellent, Mr Martin-Webber," announced Mr Rawalpindi after a while. The manager blushed with pride. "We'll get our experts to study the evidence in detail. But they're bound to reach the same conclusion as we have. Which is that the layout of this store is appalling."

BMW felt his heart skip a beat. The manager of Big B Stores in Sunny-on-Sea had been sacked just before he'd committed suicide. No connection, of course.

"It's not a problem," Alicia went on calmly. "Now we know what grabs your customers' attention, we'll be able to draw up an accurate plan for your future shelving." She waved a video in front of the manager's worried eyes. "Let's leave all these niggles behind us now. We're going to take you on a journey to a wonderful universe." She inserted the tape into the video recorder. "Relax, Bernard, close your eyes and just keep repeating: Life is Big B."

BMW did as he was told. When he opened his eyes, he saw there was a cartoon playing, a bit like a computer game. The hero of the game was a futuristic Big B Store. The camera panned above it for a moment while a sugary female voice spoke directly to the manager.

"Don't you think it's beautiful? But it's so big! You'd get lost, don't you think, Bernard? That's your first impression, isn't it?"

The manager shifted on his chair, not wanting to answer this unknown voice.

"Trust, Bernard, trust in B Corp. Let the spirit of B Corp guide you from shelf to shelf. Listen to it."

The music grew louder. It was one of those tunes you can't stop humming.

"You can't hear it, Bernard, but B Corp is talking to you. Surrender to the joy of consuming. Treat yourself."

Alicia and Mr Rawalpindi smiled at one another. B Corp bigwigs liked to call it *suggestive* music rather than subliminal messaging.

Just as his visitors were about to leave, the manager plucked up the courage to ask them about something that'd been bothering him for a while. This farting goo everybody was talking about, the one they said stained your hands and triggered hallucinations … did it really exist?

"Because if it does," he said, trying to sound confident, "you can count me out."

Alicia stared at him blandly. "A rumour is just another form of promotion. It's the customers' job to talk, Bernard, and yours to sell."

"Well, those tubs are certainly flying off the shelf," he gabbled. Then, laughing, he added, "I've even started collecting them myself. And while we're on the subject … how many different kinds are there, exactly?"

Alicia looked up at the ceiling mysteriously. "Who can tell, Bernard?"

Klaus the albino, aka Chalk Face, was furious. He'd got something to say. Something that mattered to B Corp. If they'd only rewound the CCTV video a few seconds, they'd have seen Einstein behind the socks on special offer. Yes, Einstein the computer programmer, the guy all of B Corp was trying to track down. Klaus should have stood his ground and told them who he'd recognized. But Alicia scared the living daylights out of him.

So Einstein was still in the neighbourhood. Klaus

had an old score to settle with him. His fingers could still feel the bump on his skull. A souvenir from their last encounter, in that Badach kid's flat. And to think that right now Einstein was somewhere close by. Einstein and his famous electric blue computer. Klaus's mouth twisted in a snarl of hatred. In his mind Einstein was also – above all – Sven's murderer. The man who'd left his friend to rot in the basements like a stinking rat. Who else could it have been?

Once he'd reached the first concrete towers of the Moreland Estate, Klaus started watching every passer-by, scrutinizing each face. He wouldn't leave Moreland Town without finding Einstein.

When his mobile rang he swore, thinking it was Alicia ordering him back to the black limousine.

"Yeah?" he grouched.

He didn't recognize the young voice that came out of the receiver. Wrong number, probably.

"What d'you mean, who is it?" Unbelievable!

"We're locked in," said the voice. "Come and get us!"

Klaus nearly hung up. It was probably just kids having a laugh, dialling random numbers. But then he noticed the caller's name that had flashed up on his screen, and swallowed a shout of amazement.

Sven.

"Hold on," he answered. "What did you just say?"

Klaus couldn't make much sense of the explanation that followed. But he knew he had to get to Hummingbird Tower, where Sven's mobile was in the hands of some people locked in the basements. In the basements where Sven's body had been found. Was it a trap? He made sure his gun was at the ready.

"Don't panic, my young friend," he told Samir kindly. "I'm on my way!"

Samir turned triumphantly to his teacher. "He's on his way!"

"Who? Majid?"

Samir became flustered. "Er, no, it was ... somebody."

"You don't know who it was?" yelped Sebastian. "And he's on his way? What are we going to do with the monster?"

"Hug me," suggested Joke.

"Not now," Lulu scolded. "It's best if we hide you."

Hugh agreed. At least that way they'd avoid being mobbed in the entrance hall.

Lulu kept talking to Joke as she led him back to lot 401. "Now, be good and I'll be back to find you later."

They didn't have long to wait. Klaus soon found the padlocked door. He rattled it before knocking.

"Who is it?" shouted Samir.

"Are you there, my young friend?" Klaus answered. "Are you alone?"

"No, I'm with—"

Hugh held a finger to his lips.

"—some friends."

"There isn't a grown-up with you?" asked Klaus, who was still hoping to corner Einstein.

Hugh shook his head.

"Er … nnnnnooo."

The sound of footsteps in the main entrance hall interrupted their conversation. It was the caretaker, accompanied by Brutus. The dog started growling.

"What's going on?" the caretaker asked.

"There are kids locked inside."

"What? Right!" he roared. "That's great, that is. I'm calling the police straight away."

But Klaus didn't want the police mixed up in this business. "Don't you remember me?" he said. "I'm one of the private detectives." Discreetly he slid a note out of his wallet. "I'll take care of this myself. If you'll just open the door for me…"

It happened very quickly. The note exchanged hands, and the caretaker clicked open the padlock. "Out you come, then!" he grunted.

Brutus barked and then flattened himself fearfully on the tiled floor. Klaus had his hand in his pocket, ready to draw his gun. It was probably just kids playing some stupid game, but if Einstein was there he had to catch him.

Lulu was the first to appear, looking frail and sweet under her mass of curly hair. Next came Sebastian, blinking nervously, followed by Samir, his head ducked to avoid any blows, and finally Hugh. In the gloom Klaus mistook the lanky young teacher for a teenager.

"Well, if it isn't the Ben Azet kid from the first floor," said the caretaker, recognizing Samir. "No surprises there."

Samir had had some experience of situations like this. He turned suddenly towards the basements and shouted, "Come on!"

Klaus thought somebody was still in there, reluctant to come out. And who could it be but Einstein? He headed for the door, leaving the coast clear. The caretaker was busy calming a petrified Brutus.

"Run for it!" yelled Samir.

There was a mad rush. They each went in a different direction, leaving Klaus the albino looking like a lemon.

The caretaker laughed. "You've been had. There's nobody down there." And if there is, he thought to himself as he clicked the padlock shut, well, they're done for.

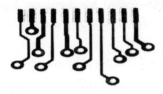

Back at Bubble's Den

Mrs Mullins didn't understand why Hugh had thrown all his tubs of farting goo in the bin. She'd managed to rescue the lids.

It was Wednesday afternoon, and she was alone in the flat. Her son had told her he'd be back for tea. She liked waiting for Hugh, because he was usually on time. She liked being able to say to herself: in ten minutes he'll be here, in five minutes…

She stood outside her son's study and hesitated briefly. Being a psychologist, she knew you should respect your child's territory, especially when your child was twenty-six years old. But she always had a good excuse: changing the water for the flowers, airing the room… In she went.

What a smell! Hugh hadn't been able to (didn't want to, clearly) explain what it was. Grumbling, she went to open the window. Then, absent-mindedly but still listening out for him, she picked up several scattered pieces of homework. Over by the computer she found a letter. The tortured, childish handwriting was Hugh's.

Can anybody love the way I love you, without expecting anything in return, without hoping for anything? You're so close, but so out of reach. I don't want to play any more. Natasha, my unreal Natasha, you're hitched to my dreams, but I'll never be able to marry you.

Mrs Mullins looked away. Hugh must have fallen in love with a married woman. Young people these days got themselves entangled in such complicated situa— Hold on, hold on! This time, she was sure. Something was moving around under the antique chest of drawers. She ran to the kitchen to fetch a broom.

Bubble had plugged himself back in. Nifty, that socket under the drawers. He fitted his recharging sessions around the comings and goings of the two other characters. His initial panic had subsided. He'd got five lives, so he could afford to relax. But he was really having to slog it out at this stage of the game.

No complaints about the graphics: the colours and shadows looked realistic enough. But the setting didn't exactly blow you away. The carpet, the swivel chair, the desk, the chest of drawers — antique, mind you — didn't do much for him. As for the babe, she was nothing to write home about. Basically, the problem at this level was that you couldn't tell what the missions were any more. OK, there were still traps. But you weren't going to catch a dragon with a mousetrap. From time to time the babe did some stick action. Without wanting to get too personal, she looked like a Teenage Mutant Ninja Turtle past its sell-by date. Bubble had no problems dodging her. She even gave a clear verbal warning before launching her attack. Like right now, in fact.

"Pssst! Shove off!"

Bubble had found all the hidey-holes on this level: under the piles of homework, along the skirting board and in a mound of socks. That last place stank, but dragons are made of stern stuff.

"Pssst! Go on, shove off!"

The babe was banging the wall. Not a very smart tactic. Bubble had escaped from under the chest of drawers ages ago. Discreetly he attacked from behind, firing a laser-precise jet of fire at her slippers. Just for fun. It only made a small row of holes. There'd been a serious bug in the game ever since the storm, and he never got a chance to destroy the Evildoers any more. He had to wait hours just to get a piece of the action.

Gangly Guy, Bubble called the other character, who'd got hair like Sonic the Hedgehog. What was the point having 3D vision, if all you saw was him marking exercise books and frowning and going "pfffff!" without even deflating?

"Go on, hop it!" squawked the babe, who'd tracked Bubble down to her son's bedroom now and was poking under the bed with her stick.

No, as far as Bubble was concerned, Golem had got off to a great start. But the game's programmers must have been high on special farting goo at this point, because it had become a total waste of time. Disgruntled, he burrowed deeper into a tunnel that looked rather like a shirtsleeve.

For her part, Mrs Mullins let go of her broom in exasperation and rubbed the small of her back. It was very crafty, this creepy-crawly. A faint – a very faint – noise like a distant humming put her on the alert again. She turned round, trying to spot where the sound was coming from. It was the printer in Hugh's study. Mrs Mullins didn't know much about technology, so she wasn't particularly surprised to see a sheet of paper coming out of the machine. She glanced at it and shuddered. On the paper were the words:

Play with me. I'm waiting for you!

And it was signed.

Natasha

"She's chasing him over the Internet now," whispered Mrs Mullins, who suspected this Natasha was a bit of a tease.

Suddenly she noticed how dark the room was getting. Dark and oppressive. The evening was starting to set in and she hadn't even noticed. She checked her watch. "Half past seven!"

Hugh had said he'd be back in time for tea. She looked around her at the faded flowers, the empty swivel chair, the pile of clothes. Why hadn't he called? Where was he? What was he doing? He only had to be a second late and she imagined the worst. To keep herself busy, she decided to have a bit of a tidy-up – there were clothes scattered all over the place. That shirt was clean. Mrs Mullins picked it up by the collar.

Back in the game again, Bubble's claws shot out and dug into the material to stop him tumbling out of the sleeve. But the babe was shaking hard, and Bubble lost his grip. He couldn't turn invisible either, or teleport himself somewhere else. He was clean out of special powers. The babe was going to get him. He slid down the tunnel. As he appeared out of the bottom of the sleeve, he flapped his wings.

Like most people, Bubble still thought he looked the same as when he was young: when he was in

Golemia, two metres tall, terrorizing whole popula-tions. He didn't realize that now he was just a pale green semi-transparent lizard. Once he'd landed on the carpet, he stood on his back legs and clawed the air with his front legs like a miniature *Tyrannosaurus rex*. The flicker from his mouth wasn't much bigger than the flame from a cigarette lighter. But the effect it had on Mrs Mullins was everything he could have hoped for. She screamed and ran out of the room.

Back in the sitting room, still clutching the shirt to her chest, Mrs Mullins wondered what she'd just seen. It was fat like a mouse, but it could fly. It was green, but a transparent green. She gave a shudder of horror and disgust. The creepy-crawly had looked at her and it had spat something. Trembling, she mopped her forehead. A sneaking suspicion occurred to her. The farting goo! Hadn't they said on TV that it triggered hallucinations? She'd han-dled the lids. Was that enough?

She looked back at the study. She thought she heard a noise, a scurrying sound. And it was getting closer. Was it the creepy-crawly? She wrung her hands. Why oh why wasn't Hugh home yet?

The sound of the key in the lock startled her. She wanted to call her son's name, but all that came out was a tiny strangled cry.

"Sorry," said Hugh. Dishevelled, sweaty and in a terrible state of overexcitement, all he could manage to say was the same thing again. "Sorry."

He couldn't explain why he was late. What he'd just experienced in the basements went beyond his wildest imaginings.

Fortunately for him, his mother was just as spaced out as he was. Her pupils dilated with fear, she watched him walk into the study. She signalled to him to stop, but it was too late. She closed her eyes, waiting for the cry of horror that was bound to follow.

"What about a cup of tea?" Hugh called out.

Bubble was back under the chest of drawers. His breath, jerky after his recent emotional roller coaster, was singeing the carpet around him.

WHAT should Majid and his friends be most scared of:
Majid's prize computer, Klaus the albino with the gun,
or the hugely powerful multinational
company B Corp?

HOW will Bubble, Joke and Natasha
cope in the real world?

And CAN Albert be trusted?

Find out in the next episode of Golem:
Natasha

Turn the page to read Chapter 1...

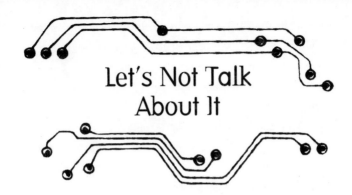

Let's Not Talk About It

There aren't many people who can keep a secret. And when it's a monstrous secret, you need to be particularly strong-minded. Hugh and his mother were both keeping a monstrous secret, because they didn't want to frighten each other.

Mrs Mullins had seen some sort of flying lizard or miniature dragon in her son's study. It had tumbled out of a sleeve when she was folding a shirt. Of course, there was nothing to stop her saying to Hugh, "Guess what? While you were out, I saw a little dragon in your study."

But somehow she couldn't see herself doing it. Being a psychologist, she'd only ever given her son sensible advice. Perhaps she could make a confession. "Guess what? I've gone mad. I keep seeing strange creatures crawling out of your shirts."

But Hugh would only say, "You should take it easy, Mum."

Mrs Mullins played and replayed the scene in her head, adding a sentence here, cutting one there. Should she blame the farting goo? After all, hadn't they said on TV there were rumours of a hallucinogenic FG? And hadn't she handled the FG tubs she'd found in Hugh's room when she was prising the lids off? Was that enough to trigger a hallucination? Mrs Mullins was clutching at straws. But as night fell, she had another idea: maybe the little dragon really did exist. At least that would account for the holes in her carpet, not to mention the odd smell.

"Don't you think there's an odd smell?" she asked at supper.

Hugh spluttered. To him nothing seemed odd right now. There was a monster in the basements of Hummingbird Tower that gave you electric shocks and talked drivel. Not only that, but the monster looked like Joke, the blob-shaped golem from his computer game. If he'd been the only one who'd seen it, Hugh would have told himself, You've gone stir-fry crazy. But there'd been three other witnesses: Sebastian, Samir and Lulu.

"No, it smells delicious," he said distractedly, sniffing his soup and dunking his fork in his bowl.

"It's easier with a spoon," said his mother.

They both laughed nervously. Hugh opened his mouth. He *had* to tell her what was going on. He couldn't carry on like this.

"Mum…"

"Yes?"

They stared at each other. Here we go, thought Mrs Mullins, he's noticed I'm going mad.

"What kind of soup is it?" asked Hugh.

"It's got carrots, potatoes, turnips," his mother recited, her voice close to breaking.

Something inside Hugh snapped. Too bad, he thought. I'm going to tell her everything. I saw a golem, I'll say. There's a golem in the basements of Hummingbird Tower.

"There's a… Are there any leeks in it?"

"Don't you like them?" she asked timidly. "You've never liked lizards very much."

"What?"

Mrs Mullins turned pale. "Did I ... did I just say something ludicrous?"

"You mentioned lizards."

"No, I said 'ludicrous'."

"Ludicrous? Weird!"

They both laughed shakily. Keeping their secrets was driving them mad.

"I'm going to visit my sister in Sunny-on-Sea," Mrs Mullins suddenly announced.

"When?"

"Tomorrow. I need a rest. Yes. A rest will do me good." There were tears in her eyes. She was deserting him. Abandoning her son to the claws of a dragon. Just as well it was only twenty centimetres tall.

"But ... will you be away long?"

"Probably a week. Will you be all right without me?"

Hugh nodded. But he knew he'd never survive on his own in the flat, with only a computer that switched itself on for company. He had to talk to somebody. Majid? Samir? Sebastian? They were just kids.

"Albert," he whispered.

"What?" asked his mother.

They looked at each other. They were on the verge of blurting everything out, but they just couldn't do it.

"I've … I've got to do some reading for an evening class. It's about Albert," stammered Hugh. "Albert Einstein."

He got up from the table, even though he'd hardly touched his soup. Yes, that was it, he needed to speak to Albert, the fugitive who claimed to have invented Golem.

"But where is he?" he wondered, half to himself and half out loud.

"In your study," answered Mrs Mullins.

"What?"

"There's a B Smart book on Einstein in your study." Atomic bombs and dragons. Mrs Mullins mopped her brow. "I'm going to bed."

Alone in his study, Hugh glanced fearfully at his electric blue computer. After clearing out his wallet, Albert had said, "If I need to get hold of you, I'll email."

Maybe he had. But Hugh didn't dare click on the Outlook Express icon to pick up his messages. He stroked the mouse softly. The screen quivered and an image popped up. His favourite.

"Well, *hello* there!"

Natasha was on the screen in flirt mode, her hands resting coyly on her hips. Hugh traced the girl-golem's outline with his finger: her mouth, her breasts, her bare thighs. He blinked. He could hardly see her for tears.

"Well, *hello* there!" she repeated.

"Oh, be quiet." Hugh flopped into his chair, reached over to the printer and grabbed the piece of paper there.

Play with me. I'm waiting for you!

His mother claimed the printer had started working of its own accord. Mrs Mullins muddled up faxes and emails, so she hadn't been particularly alarmed. But Hugh knew that messages didn't spontaneously appear from an ordinary printer. It was even signed.

Natasha

Had Albert invented a game whose characters could interact with the real world? It was ridiculous. Unthinkable. But Joke was in the basements of Hummingbird Tower right now, blowing all the fuses to satisfy his appetite for electricity. It was ridiculous. Impossible!

"Ridiculous," Hugh whispered, eyes glued to Natasha. A crazy idea was forming. If Joke had escaped from the game, why couldn't Natasha? Hugh caressed the flat image with the back of his hand. She was his adolescent dream, the girl who'd haunted his fantasies at a time when his friends had teased him for being a wimp.

Natasha's curves were designed to make super-models green with envy. She was wasp-waisted, her eyes were somewhere between gold and emerald, and her mouth looked like it was always being kissed. With her girl-warrior's frame, pneumatic breasts and eraser-laser slung across her shoulder, she could seduce anybody and kill anybody too. But her creator had failed in one thing: when Hugh had clicked on *obedient* for her character, he'd got stuck with *aggressive*. Albert hadn't had time to fine-tune certain details of the game, and, worse still, he hadn't had time to finish it. What was the point of playing with the girl-golem if she couldn't gain a soul from the Master Golem at the end of her quest?

But Hugh's fondness for Natasha eventually conquered his fear, and he gave the mouse a nudge. "Are you in an aggressive mood?" he asked.

The image jumped. Natasha seized her weapon and aimed it at the outside world. Directly at Hugh. Instinctively he swivelled back in his chair.

"Calm down!"

But she had already turned her back on him and was heading off down an unknown path. Hugh had never seen this part of the game before. Had Albert lied? Had he led Natasha to the Master Golem after all? The girl-golem was striding confidently along under a magnificently starry sky.

One of the stars started flashing, then got bigger. Bigger and bigger. Hugh blinked. It had filled the screen and was twinkling from all five points, as brightly as the star above the manger in Bethlehem. There was a little square in each point. By now, Hugh was familiar with the rattling sound of an old typewriter that came through the speakers. The following words appeared on the screen:

I am that which is known by another name.

Hugh whispered the riddle. He moved his cursor and clicked randomly on the little empty boxes. They flashed in turn, but nothing happened.

"That which is known by another name?" he wondered out loud.

He was hooked. He'd forgotten all about the nightmare earlier this afternoon. Once again, Golem was sending him on a journey. But where to? Could *that which is* be the Master Golem, the god of the game? You probably had to type a letter in each box to form a kind of password.

"Five letters," muttered Hugh. He had to screen his eyes from the glare of the star. Suddenly the image disappeared, as if the game was fed up of waiting.

He decided to check his emails. Had Albert been trying to get in touch? A blue figure in brackets showed there were twelve new messages in Hugh's in-box. And all twelve were from Albert, care of Cyberstation, an Internet café in Moreland Town.

Hugh opened the last one.

> Jeez, don't you ever check your emails?
> I have to see you. I'll be at Cyb every
> afternoon this week. Get over here, or
> I'll turn up at your place.

Hugh smiled faintly. I expect you need more money, my friend, he thought. Let's make a deal. The money for the password.